Acclaim for *The Shovel and the Loom*

"In *The Shovel and the Loom*, Carl Friedman perfectly accomplishes the delicate task of making unspeakable stories at once accessible and shocking."
—Katherine Alberg, *The New York Times Book Review*

"One thing is certain: [Friedman's] vivid emotional power. Her prose is spare and reticent and her narrative gifts impressive. Among the emerging voices of the second generation of Holocaust survivors she deserves high rank."
—Robert Taylor, *The Boston Globe*

"A deceptively simply story that captures with astounding clarity a young woman's search for meaning and humanity in the shadow of her parents' Holocaust experience. [Carl Friedman] is an artist of enormous talent."
—Sharon Pomerantz, *Hadassah Magazine*

"[Carl Friedman's] latest novel tells an exquisite and harrowing tale.... Chaya's troubles, both private and universal, resonate long after the end of this bewitching book."
—Carolyn Alessio, *Chicago Tribune*

"A powerful and moving work, containing moments of humor despite its tragic elements, *The Shovel and the Loom* is a fitting successor to *Nightfather*."  —Gabriel Motola, *San Francisco Chronicle*

"Throughout the novel Friedman uses Jewish learning in illuminating ways....[She] successfully transcends her own ~~aut-~~ raphy to create a fictional world ~~tha~~
post-Holocaust imagination."
—Judith B

ALSO BY CARL FRIEDMAN

*Nightfather*

*The Gray Lover*

DISCARD

The
SHOVEL
and the
LOOM

Carl Friedman

*Translated from the Dutch by Jeannette K. Ringold*

*A Karen and Michael Braziller Book*
PERSEA BOOKS | | NEW YORK

Originally published under the title *Twee koffers vol* in 1993
by Uitgeverij G.A. van Oorschot, Amsterdam.
First published in the United States of America in 1996
by Persea Books, New York.

*For information, write to the publisher:*

*Persea Books, Inc.
171 Madison Avenue
New York, New York 10016*

*The publisher gratefully acknowledges the financial support
of the Dutch Literary Foundation.*

Poetry by Heinrich Heine on page 156 is reprinted from
*The Complete Poems of Heinrich Heine: A Modern English Version*,
by Hal Draper (Suhrkamp/Insel Publishers, Boston, 1982).
Used by permission of Suhrkamp Verlag, Frankfurt.

*Library of Congress Cataloging-in-Publication Data*

Friedman, Carl.
    [Twee koffers vol. English]
    The shovel and the loom / Carl Friedman : translated from the
Dutch by Jeannette K. Ringold.
    p.   cm.
    ISBN 0-89255-216-6 (hardcover)
    ISBN 0-89255-231-X (paperback)
    I. Ringold, Jeannette K.  II. Title.
    PT5881.16.R48T8513  1996
    839.3'1364—dc20                                      95-53825
                                                              CIP

Designed by REM Studio, Inc.
Typeset in Cochin by Keystrokes, Lenox, Massachusetts
Manufactured in the United States of America

First paperback printing

*The*

SHOVEL

*and the*

LOOM

**T**he one photograph I have from that time tells me little that I don't already know. The face supported by my hands is familiar enough. But the noncommittal look in my eyes betrays nothing of what preoccupied me then, let alone the strange events that were to follow. It could be a photograph of anyone at any time, except for a small detail that, as details often do, reveals the truth. Behind the window framing my head there is a vague outline of something that obviously was moving during the exposure and that I recognize with great difficulty as the high breast of a pigeon. The pigeons! They populated Antwerp as naturally as did its citizens. Even in the rain gutter under my window they stupidly cooed and pattered about nervously at the crack of dawn.

I was twenty years old then and studying philosophy. As soon as I had registered at the university, I no longer wanted to live with my parents. Philosophers, I felt, could thrive only in isolation. So I moved to the southern, run-down part of the city and found a small apartment for a bargain price. But since the rent still exceeded my modest scholarship, I had to find another source of income. In order to lead the secluded life of a philosopher, I was forced to turn to poorly paid labor. I hardly found time to attend lectures.

Mornings I worked in a flower shop known for its funeral wreaths. In a greenhouse behind the store, I stuck great quantities of flowers, their stems wound with wire, into straw forms. For standard wreaths, carnations with broken stems were used; for those of children, mostly roses. I decorated the finished wreaths with gold imprinted ribbons. Next of kin could choose from texts varying from a simple "In memoriam" to "Your easy chair is empty in front of the hearth." In this way I helped prepare a decent burial for three or so bodies daily.

After that, from the afternoon until mid-evening, I washed dishes in a large restaurant. The special attraction of this restaurant was dessert. Patrons who ordered the daily special could, to finish up, eat as much rice pudding with cherries as they wanted. Since each new portion was served on a clean plate, a large number of the dishes consisted of dessert plates that were stuck together so completely that I had to pry them apart with a knife.

The dishwashing part of the kitchen was small and crawling with cockroaches, which like to be nice and warm. They skittered across the floor, the walls, and the ceiling. They had even piled up in the lighted wall clock so that the lower half of the clock face was obscured and could not be read. As the afternoon progressed, the steamy space looked more and more like a Turkish bath. I took off my sweater and bent over the steaming sinks in an undershirt. In the end I was forced to turn on the fan. As soon as the enormous blades above my head started to whirl, roaches blew about my ears. For months I angrily knocked them off my bare shoulders and from my face. One afternoon, when a mountainous landscape of sticky dishes was taking shape in the sink and I had twice brushed a crawling cockroach from my lips, I quit on the spot. It was January.

During the weeks that followed I went to the university in the afternoon. That was no luxury; examinations were coming up soon. Since the orals would be given in a common room where our professors would have their own table but no name plate, I urgently needed to get to know them by sight. Of course, upon entering the hall, I could call out, "Which one of you is Professor Klinkers?" Or "Would Professor Van Averbeke please raise his hand?" But I understood that this would not be to my advantage.

I couldn't make ends meet with my earnings from the flower shop. In order to buy newspapers, magazines, and, once in a while, a book, I saved money on food. At the end of March the situation became serious. In my kitchen cabinet there remained only a package of margarine, a partly used tube of tomato puree, and three eggs. I had no choice but to eat a tomato-flavored omelet. Then I went to read my landlady's paper. In the Help Wanted section I found an ad in which a "promeneuse" was urgently wanted.

"A cushy job," said my landlady. "All you have to do is push a baby carriage through the park and you get paid." It seemed to me that no special qualifications were needed for steering a baby carriage. I didn't have the slightest experience with children, but they simply had to be more agreeable than cockroaches. This is how it came about that I went in good spirits to report to Mrs. Kalman, who had placed the ad.

Above the dome of Central Station, the sky was clear

blue. Humming, and with the *Antwerp Gazette* under my arm, I walked into Pelikaan Street. Here begins what is popularly called the "Jewish quarter," a district not inhabited exclusively by Jews but where Jews do determine the street scene. In their distinctive dress they still give that part of the city a character that, ever since the catastrophe caused by Hitler, has practically disappeared from Europe. Because in this district life is governed by centuries-old traditions, the people of Antwerp maintain that here time stands still. Perhaps that is true. But I know of no other place where stand-ing still is epitomized by as much movement as here, in little Warsaw, where I spent my youth.

I passed Hasidim in caftans and fur hats, who were engaged in heated discussions with one another. Housewives argued loudly with shopkeepers. Near the Diamond Exchange, groups of men deliberated on the sidewalk. Behind their glasses sparkled nearsighted eyes. Some wore sidecurls and a beard, others were shaven, but all wore the traditional black hat. I imag-ined how an expert acrobat, stepping from one hat to the next, might be able to travel Olympic distances over their heads.

In Simons Street, I walked under the railroad tracks. Three Hasidic pre-schoolers came toward me. With their dark caps they seemed to be coming from a faraway, mysterious Polish shtetl. Their faces were dead serious, and they held each other tightly by the hand, as though around the next corner the men from Pilsudski could be lying in ambush. Not for anything in the world did I want to be the cause of their having to let go of each other. When I stepped aside to let them pass, I heard someone call my name. I turned around and stood face to face with old Mr. Apfelschnitt. My parents lived nearby, and he was their upstairs neighbor. In spite of his seventy-five years, he went through life with a perfectly straight back. He didn't walk, he strode. The children of the neighborhood used to call him, whispering, the King of Lange Kievit Street and would bow when he passed by. With his broad shoulders, his high forehead, and his searching gaze, he was quite an authoritative presence. But I, who had been at his house since I was a child, knew that he possessed the sort of gentleness that only the truly strong can allow themselves.

"Will you walk with me?" he asked, offering me his arm.

"No, not today."

"You seldom come home these days," he said. "Remember the fifth commandment."

"I can honor my father and mother just as well from a distance."

"Yes, but then it shouldn't surprise you that they

don't notice it much. How are your studies?"

I shrugged my shoulders and said, "I wish I knew. The more I read, the less I understand everything. Perhaps I should have chosen another direction, something with more substance. Philosophy is not practical. What's the use of staring through your window at the sky and wondering about the origin of the universe? It's probably a lot more sensible to conduct soil research on the moon."

He nodded. "Well, it is simply not possible in an occasional spare hour to get to the bottom of mysteries over which scholars have been puzzling for a few thousand years . . ."

"That's precisely the point," I interrupted him excitedly. "These so-called scholars are just making random guesses. Most philosophers don't know any more than you or I, Mr. Apfelschnitt. Where do we come from? Was a divine father or a slimy amoeba at our cradle? Why do we live? And if we truly aspire to good, how is it that we cause so much misery? According to Plautus, man is a wolf. According to Spengler, Darwin, and Schopenhauer, people's actions are determined by blind passions. What does that yield? A world filled with cave dwellers who on the one hand knock in each other's skull for a bite of food and on the other hand reproduce like crazy in order to preserve the species from extinction." I lowered my voice and beat my chest. "Me Tarzan," I said, "you Jane!"

Mr. Apfelschnitt frowned. "Is that all you are learning? Is that why they have to create a whole university? Tarzan you can also see at the movies." He shook his head and continued. "There will always remain mysteries. Soil research on the moon won't change that one bit. Men like Planck and Einstein have split up the world into such tiny little pieces that we have long ago lost our grasp of it. It only increases the wonder. Creation is a masterpiece. Science can never replace God or the Torah."

"And if you happen not to be religious?"

"Even atheists were created by the Almighty," said Mr. Apfelschnitt, "whether they like it or not. And the Torah applies to them as it does to everyone. Are they permitted to murder? No, that is forbidden. Shouldn't they love their neighbor? Should they not seek justice? They most certainly should. God's word is universal and eternally binding. There exists no better proof of His power."

"Nevertheless, His commandments are broken every day," I said, pointing to the houses across the way. "While we're standing here talking, behind one of those walls a father may be kicking his child crippled, or a man and a woman are driving each other crazy. God, with all His power, doesn't seem able to prevent that. Or perhaps He simply doesn't care?"

"Nonsense," declared Mr. Apfelschnitt. "Would He elevate good into law if evil left Him indifferent?" He shivered. "I'm catching a cold standing here," he muttered reproachfully, as though he wanted to say that I was wasting his time.

But as I was saying goodbye, he grabbed the sleeve of my coat.

"You really should go home again some time," he said with a commanding look. "It's your father."

"What's the matter with him?"

"Nothing, or actually all sorts of things. He's so busy nowadays that he doesn't even have time left for a game of chess with me."

"What keeps him so busy?"

"You'll have to ask him that yourself," said Mr. Apfelschnitt as he courteously touched his hat and continued on his way.

**I** crossed Plantin-Moretus Avenue and found the house number from the ad. The door was open. A man in a brown work coat was busy sweeping the entry hall. As I was looking for the doorbell, he raised his head.

"Are you supposed to be here?" he asked, suspiciously. He had a bony face, mousy hair, and a narrow mustache.

I nodded. "Yes, I'm looking for the Kalman family."

"Fourth floor." He pointed, avoiding my eyes. "Through the hall and up the stairs. There is an elevator, but it's stuck somewhere again. That's how it goes all day. People take the elevator, step out, and feel that they're too good to close the gate behind them. So you can push the button as hard as you want to, but the thing won't come down."

I climbed the bare stairs, convinced that Mr. Apfelschnitt was wrong. If the world is governed by a God who is so powerful that He can change the course of history, why does He remain aloof? In *Time* magazine I had read an article about a new weapon that the American army was using in Indo-China: a fragmentation bomb that upon exploding fired thousands of projectiles. Spiral-shaped and half a centimeter in diameter, they could destroy a life in a few seconds by penetrating deep into the flesh of people and animals. Next to the article, there was a picture of a Vietnamese baby whose head was pierced by such a projectile, causing not only blindness but permanent brain damage as well. You saw them everywhere, pictures of burning huts and farmers who had been turned into living torches by napalm. On opening the newspaper, the smoke of charred bodies would overwhelm you. What kind of God would remain indifferent to the suffering of His creation and yet was so highly regarded in the eyes of the masses? What had earned Him their admiration? The fact that in a distant past He had parted a sea and let manna fall from heaven? I thought that was a roundabout way to influence the course of history. One single miracle would have sufficed, making all others superfluous: He could have given people compassion.

The second floor smelled like fried chicken livers. The third floor seemed uninhabited. There was no longer a door but just a hole through which, in passing, I could see broken furniture. Once I reached the top floor, I rang the bell. As Mrs. Kalman let me in, she yelled something over her shoulder in the direction of her children who were elsewhere in the apartment making too much noise to hear her. "*Seit shtill,* be quiet!" she screamed. Later I would often hear that shout. She screamed strictly for form's sake.

After I had introduced myself and had waved the newspaper with the ad, she motioned me to the living room. In it there stood only a worn sofa with matching chairs and a table. On the table there was a blue velvet bag of the kind Jewish men use to store their prayer straps. Nothing hung on the walls except a narrow, embroidered runner that indicated east, the direction in which Orthodox Jews turn to say their daily prayers. Right behind the windows there was chicken wire, about chest-high: to prevent the children from falling out, or to keep the world from entering? The fenced-in view oppressed me.

Mrs. Kalman did not invite me to sit down but, standing, asked me my age.

"I'm twenty," I said, "and a student."

Her glance went from my worn jacket to my jeans.

She herself wore a high-buttoned blouse, a skirt, and dark stockings with pumps. She had pale cheeks and pale lips, which made her face look like a marble bust from antiquity. But her eyes were dark and sensitive. I guessed her to be in her early thirties. She looked older because of her *shaytl*, the wig that Orthodox Jewish women wear over their own hair, according to a centuries-old custom.

"What do you study?"

"Philosophy."

She raised her eyebrows. "And to practice philosophy you have to wear pants?"

"My legs get cold when I wear a skirt," I said.

"I assume that your brains are not in your knees," she said mocking. "It's impossible for you to come to work here in these clothes. We live *frum*. A woman should not disguise herself as a man; that is contrary to the Torah."

I wanted to say that I moved in enlightened circles where a woman was recognized as such, even when wearing pants. But I urgently needed to find work and couldn't afford to be critical. Fortunately, Mrs. Kalman didn't come back to this matter, not even the next day when I started work in that very disguise. Inside the house she had me wear an apron over my jeans. It was an old-fashioned model with puffed sleeves. The pockets were soon heavy with clothes pins, safety pins, pacifiers, and bibs, for my landlady had been wrong: I was not paid just to stroll through the park.

Of the five children in the Kalman family, eight-year-old Avrom and six-year-old Dov went to school, so that I didn't see them until late in the afternoon. My task consisted mainly of taking care of the twin sisters Tzivya and Esha, who were five months old. That was not simple. While I was giving a bottle to Tzivya , Esha shrieked with hunger. And when I changed Esha's diaper, Tzivya was crying in her cradle. Finally, struggling with little sleeves and bows, I managed to put sweaters on the children. Then I would bring the collapsible frame of the carriage to the ground floor. After that, I would drag the wide body of the carriage, which didn't fit in the narrow elevator with me, down the stairs. This done, one after the other, I picked up the baby girls, who were usually crying and who didn't quiet down until the carriage started moving. The work took much out of me. The fact that I didn't quit after a few days was solely because of Simcha Kalman.

Simcha Kalman was the youngest of the boys. His name, which means "joy" in Hebrew, seemed hardly suitable for him. Whenever his brothers rough-housed, Simcha would watch quietly and at a distance. Avrom and Dov had luxuriant curly hair, with sidecurls that framed their olive-colored cheeks like black brackets. Simcha's hair was a dull red and so thin that his skull was visible through it, as though he were already becoming bald in his toddler years. His sidecurls hung straight down on either side of his splotchy face.

I loved him immediately, as soon as his mother pulled him out of the gray plush armchair where he had hidden during our first meeting. "This is Simcha," she said, pushing him forward. "He is almost four and he still wets his pants."

Simcha was indeed not yet toilet trained, but I didn't mind changing him. Usually, he got soaked through to his *tallit katan*, the prayer shirt with fringes that Orthodox boys wear under their outer clothing from the moment that they master the language suffi- ciently to say a prayer. The wet clothes were stiff, but Simcha subjected himself calmly to my clumsy tugging. Contemptuously, his brothers called him "pickled her- ring" because of the urine smell that soap could no longer wash out of his clothes.

As I pushed the carriage with the twins on board to the park, I kept one hand free. Holding on to that hand, Simcha walked along with me. I spoke to him in Yiddish, because he understood no other language. He seldom said anything in reply. During our walk he didn't look up at me. He looked straight ahead. The world emptied into his pale blue eyes. With great seriousness, he took things in. His small head under the woollen cap became heavy with them.

But once we reached the pond in the park, a great joy came over him. "Ducks," he said emphatically and let go of my hand. Weightless, he danced along the water's edge. He became especially excited at seeing a duck turn upside down like an acrobat and dunk its head underwater. Shouting with laughter, he pointed to the curled tail feathers on the rump that stuck straight up in the air. His thin lips disappeared in his face. I put the brake on the baby carriage and went to sit on one of the benches along the path. There I waited until, forgetting himself, he came to me and pushed his head into my arms. For me, he was the sweetest and the most beautiful. Even at night, while I was bent over my books in my rented room, he remained in my thoughts. In the margin of a textbook on metaphysical rationalism, I wrote the Hebrew letters *sin, mem, chet,* and *hay,* which together formed his name and which in their angularity distracted my attention from scholastic and Cartesian structures. Around it I drew ducks.

r. Apfelschnitt was right. Although it was a walk of only half an hour to my parents' house, I seldom went there. My mother was especially distressed by this. "You are all we have," she often sighed. That was not true. Aside from me, she had a group of women friends who regularly came for tea and who drove my recently retired father crazy with their gossip.

My mother was the daughter of a tailor who had sent his seven children to the best schools. Whenever she dipped pieces of bread in her coffee at the breakfast table, she would say apologetically, "I know that dunking isn't proper, but I can't resist." She valued good manners and considered me too unrestrained and ill-mannered. I talked too animatedly and my gestures were too emphatic. "Easy, easy," she would say imploringly, as soon as I opened my mouth. As a child I was constantly reined in by her. "That one," she'd often say to my father, pointing in my direction, "burns up twice as fast as anyone else." At one point he'd had enough. *"Meg sein,"* he said casually, "but she also gives off twice as much light!"

He was tall and limber. My mother claimed that she could recognize him in a street crowded with a hundred people by his way of walking. "He moves from his hips," she said proudly. "Other men don't have that, they don't leave the ground." He did indeed make a boyish impression. Whenever he'd stick his hand in his pocket, you expected bits of string, wild chestnuts, and soccer cards to appear. In the thirties, having fled from Berlin to Brussels, he worked as a dance teacher to finance his study of mathematics. Tap dancing was his specialty. He had been in the cast of a movie directed by a filmmaker who had also fled Germany. Although he was one of many dancers in the background, as a child I imagined that even Fred Astaire could not hold a candle to him.

My mother, many years younger than he, had met him in the summer of 1947. She liked to talk about it. "It was terribly hot. I was wearing a white suit that looked black because it was covered with midges. And I was wearing a blue pillbox hat. How did I manage to get it? It was adorable, with red ribbons that tied under my chin." My father asked her out to a restaurant where she ordered a meal of six courses, consisting of as many servings of ice cream. Afterward he had kissed her in the middle of the street. Whenever she got to this part of the story, he would call out, "I had no choice. I had to defrost you!" She never talked about the years 1940–45. The little I knew of her life during the war was told to me by my father who had only a vague inkling of it.

When I had worked at the Kalmans for almost two weeks, I finally went to visit my parents. I went there after work and had to walk only two blocks to get there. Although evening was falling, I still heard the tom-tom of carpet-beaters everywhere. With the Passover holiday approaching, the giant ritual cleaning had spread through the neighborhood like a plague. During the eight days of Passover Jews are forbidden to eat or drink anything containing any leavening whatsoever, and even the smallest trace of yeast has to disappear from Jewish homes. Housewives had been busy for several weeks hunting for stale bread crumbs and preparing their households for the commemoration of the exodus from Egypt. They scrubbed and polished, beat and swept. Nothing remained in its place. In the twilight, carpets were airing on every balcony like dark flags. Here and there, furniture was standing in the street, as though its owners were packing their belongings in order to follow Moses once again to the promised land.

In my parents' apartment there also reigned an atmosphere of excitement. My father was sitting at the table, writing. Next to his stationery, several stamped envelopes lay ready. He seemed nervous.

My mother talked about one thing and another. Did I know that near them a new greengrocer which sold rotten apples had opened? Had I heard that wearing tight jeans could cause cancer? Had a neighbor who'd seen me pushing a baby carriage in Stadspark mistaken someone else for me?

"I have a new recipe for cake," she told me. "I used to beat the whole eggs into the batter; now I use only the yolks. I keep the egg whites separate and beat them stiff. I don't add them until the last moment. This way the cake is a lot lighter, but I wonder whether it's at the expense of smoothness." Reluctantly I let myself be led to the kitchen.

"Just taste," she said. Then she closed the door behind us and whispered, "Did you see that? He's writing letters to half the world. And he has a map that he's marking with crosses!"

"So?" I said, with my mouth full of cake. "I draw ducks in my philosophy books."

"Perhaps," she said, "but you aren't sixty yet. That's a bit old for such nonsense. He's looking for things he buried during the war. Two suitcases full of stuff, at the other end of the city. I'm trying to talk him out of it, but he can't think of anything else. Every day he's gone for hours, and when he returns home he starts writing letters." She came closer to me. "What do you think of it?"

"Does it matter what I think of it? If he really wants to play detective, it's up to him."

"No," she said, "I mean the cake. Isn't it on the dry side?"

"It's good."

"Just as good as usual?"

I nodded, but she looked doubtful.

"It could still be a little smoother, don't you think? Perhaps it was better with the whole eggs in it."

"Yes, now that you mention it," I answered, to humor her.

No one who heard my mother fuss about the eggs in her cake could have imagined that when she was my age she had been harnessed like a donkey to a cart that she had to pull along the streets of Auschwitz. Wasn't her attention to frivolities the ultimate denial of all that?

Look at me, she seemed to be saying, I can afford to talk about trivialities; nothing is wrong with me.

When we returned to the living room, my father had put away his writing materials. He told me all about the suitcases. How he had taken them along to his first hiding place, a temporary shelter, where he could stay only one night. How he was told that the next morning he would be brought to a safer address, outside the city. The trip there would be long and would be made by bicycle. Not only were the suitcases too heavy to be transported in that way, but also he would be too conspicuous with them. Therefore my father wanted to leave them behind in the house in question. But his host wasn't exactly eager to be appointed as keeper of the possessions of a person who was on the wanted list of the Gestapo. So it happened that he, together with my father, had buried the suitcases in the backyard at dusk.

"What was in them?" I asked.

My father was clearly happy with that question. "Mostly books," he told me, "but I don't remember which ones. And my old violin, of course. There is also an antique top in the shape of a dancer. Her skirt is made of small iron rods that jingle when she turns. And there's a photo album."

It struck me that he spoke about the contents in the present tense, as though the missing suitcases could at any moment come within reach. But why had he waited so long before beginning the search?

"I didn't procrastinate," he said, "it just didn't occur to me. After the war you had to go forward. Whoever looked back turned into a pillar of salt."

My mother intervened in the discussion. "That quarter has been completely redeveloped," she said implacably. "A colossal five-story parking garage has been built there. But your father lets nothing stop him. He's ready to tear down the city with his own hands in order to find his suitcases."

He ignored her. "I have written letters to the councilman in charge of town planning," he told me, "and to the city archives. If I can get a detailed map of the old and the new plans, then it will be a snap to locate my suitcases."

"Let the past be," said my mother. "Those books have long ago turned into pulp. And moles are living in your violin."

"What would you know about that?" my father said, irritated. "There's a good chance that everything has been saved and is ready to be picked up. I especially want the photos. My parents are in them. And Selma."

We had no photographs of my grandfather and grandmother. We had a few of my aunt Selma, but only from the years after the war when she was a piano teacher in the Musikschule in Frankfurt. Those were group portraits in which she, slight and timid, was surrounded by a flock of colleagues. They were like picture puzzles: Where is Aunt Selma? As a child, it was always difficult for me to find her. Most likely she herself had the same problem, for one evening she committed suicide by drinking hot chocolate containing a strong barbiturate. When this happened, I was twelve years old. My father traveled to Frankfurt to arrange the funeral, while my mother remained at home. Shaking her head, she said, "Hot chocolate! What could she have been thinking of?" As though my aunt had sinned against etiquette, as if the usual custom was to mix barbiturates into clear vegetable soup, or to serve them with cinnamon and sugar.

On hearing the name Selma, we lapsed into a gloomy silence. Finally my mother said softly, "What do you think you'll find in those photos? A person is who he is, not who he has been."

Later that evening, after I had said goodbye and was walking home through the deserted neighborhood, I thought back to her words. She was wrong. A person was most certainly who he had been. I stopped at the darkened window of a kosher restaurant. It used to be the store of Teitelbaum, the hunchbacked druggist, who was known for his miserliness. People said that his hump wasn't of flesh and blood but consisted of all the money he had scraped together throughout his life and from which he could not be parted for a moment, so that he had to carry it always on his back. As children, in the summer we would press the sticky paper from our ice cream bars against his shop window. Then he would come out and, cursing, chase us, all the while holding his hat down on his head with both hands. One time he was so close on my heels that he would certainly have grabbed me, but I was saved by Shrulik the ragman, who lifted me through the air, put me in his pushcart, and quickly ran away with me. Turning around, I saw how Teitelbaum still raged and spat with anger. Strands of saliva glistened in his thin beard. Shrulik laughed. My mother had strictly forbidden me to go with Shrulik. She said that he stank like a nest of mice. And perhaps that was so, but we loved the old man, and after school we crowded around him. Sometimes he let five of us at the same time climb onto his cart. There we'd sit, on top of the rags, while he, like a croaking horn, would call out, *"Kinder, shayne kinder!"* as though he were offering us for sale.

One day, Shrulik was dead. A neighbor woman said that he had been one hundred twenty years old, just like Moses. Not only had I believed it then, but I was still willing to believe it. Standing in front of the empty restaurant, I missed Shrulik desperately. Suddenly I understood very well why my father was ready to go to any lengths to retrieve a couple of suitcases with moldy memories. I myself wouldn't hesitate for a moment to dig up the long-dead Shrulik if that were possible. I would help him to his feet, change his shroud for his worn black coat, and brush a clump of earth from his beard just to see him push his cart loaded with rags over the cobblestones one more time. And then, just as before on raw days, the wind would blow his sidecurls upward, as though his hat were sprouting wings.

I continued walking and turned the corner. A human being was not only who he had been but also with whom and where he had been. He was the words he had heard and the voices with which they had been spoken; he was the images he had seen, the smells he had smelled, and all the hands that had touched him. My mother might say that the past has no importance, but why was she forever busy exorcising it? Every day, all over again, she had to bury Auschwitz under cake recipes and teas: reverse archaeology. No wonder she opposed my father's plans. She feared that in digging for his suitcases he would expose her Pompeii.

A s long as Mrs. Kalman gave no evidence to the contrary, I assumed she was satisfied with my work. She continued to address me formally, as Miss. She politely ignored every attempt I made to start a conversation. Would she rather not hear details about my way of life, which according to her views had to be immoral? Or was she just too busy? While I was taking care of the twins and Simcha, she spent hours working in the kitchen.

Even so, she found time for study and prayer. In the afternoon, when I returned from my walk with the children, she was often praying. On the kitchen table the *korban mincha* lay open, between stacks of folded laundry. From this prayer book for women she read aloud. But, when she heard us come in, her sing-song Hebrew would stop. She'd finish the prayer and snap her book shut. She pressed her lips passionately to the worn cover before putting it away. Then she would tie her apron on again and resume her work.

Because of their household tasks, Jewish women are freed from obligatory prayers. How could they retreat into prayer three times a day as men do? Whining children would cling to their skirts, food would boil over, and the house would grow dirty. But a daughter of Israel does not have an easy life. From her childhood on, she must compete with the righteous matriarchs from Holy Scripture. There is an extensive literature containing rules of conduct for the Jewish woman. That literature emphasizes a certain humility. For example, it mentions not "diligence" but "quiet diligence," not "love" but "modest love." Words like *discreet* and *modest* are the order of the day. Screaming and the slamming of doors are not included.

Most of these books refer to the last chapter of Proverbs: praise of the woman of valor. This verse, which seems more like an exhortation than a hymn of praise, sums up all the virtues that a righteous wife should possess according to biblical mores. Her lamp does not go out at night. She does her husband good and not evil, all the days of her life. She is filled with trembling respect for the Almighty. And if that weren't enough, she should also be faithful and wise, vigilant and industrious. If she succeeds in this, the Proverbs promise that her name will be praised even at the gates of the City.

Although Mrs. Kalman abided scrupulously by the rules, she was anything but subservient. She did what was expected of her with authority and self-confidence. The shabby apartment was a fort that she manned all alone and defended against the evil outside world. On her shoulders rested the heavy task of raising the children in the Hasidic tradition and of maintaining the Jewish dietary laws. I felt a certain respect, not so much for the laborious way in which she strictly applied these laws, but for the fact that in doing this she never for a moment was tempted to doubt the value of a kosher household. I understood that even the smallest actions that she carried out as a matter of fact in front of her stove were more important for Judaism than the weighty pronouncements of any chief rabbi. What would happen to tradition if there weren't an army of housewives like Mrs. Kalman who, by stirring, beating, baking, and roasting, elevated the law to practice? The sturdiest basis of Jewish orthodoxy seemed to consist of chicken soup with kreplach, gefilte fish, borscht, bulbenik, and so much kugel that after the meal no one thought of committing sins, simply because no one could get up out of his chair.

When Mrs. Kalman wasn't cooking, she was ironing or sewing. Sitting behind an ancient Singer treadle sewing machine, she made her husband and sons shirts that were closed not with buttons but with ribbons, according to the practice of the Hasidic sect to which the family belonged. On the collar she embroidered, in white on white, delicate Hebrew designs. In addition she had to do much mending, for the Kalmans were not rich. My salary was therefore meager as well. It was paid to me on Friday, just before the beginning of Shabbat, by Mr. Kalman.

I was in the dark about Mr. Kalman's occupation. From the few comments of his wife I gathered that he was a merchant, but I hadn't the faintest idea of what. Of chocolate? This seemed plausible, because every Friday together with my salary he also gave me two large bars of Swiss chocolate, and because he regularly traveled to Bern. But it was just as likely that he went there to make bulk purchases of Emmenthaler cheese, watches, or aspirin.

Mr. Kalman was not tall, but his heavy-set figure in a black caftan made a solid impression. His square-shaped face was slightly rounded by light brown side-curls and a frizzy beard. He had a voice like sandpaper, but he never used it to speak to me. Silently he walked past me in the house and silently he laid my weekly salary on the table. I knew that his Orthodox lifestyle forbade him to touch women other than his wife and that it was therefore impossible for him to place the money directly into my hands. But nowhere in the holy books was it written that he could not speak to me. I considered his silence a sign of disdain.

He did speak to his children, although even then he wasn't lavish with words. Usually he brought them into line with gruff commands, for in his eyes they did much wrong. Once, when I had pulled off Simcha's wet clothes and was helping him into clean pants, we were startled by Mr. Kalman's rasping Yiddish. Threatening, he pointed to the raised left leg of his youngest son while shouting, "How often do I have to repeat? First the right leg, the right one!" What was wrong with the left leg? He looked at it as though it were infected with leprosy.

"It's my fault," I said nervously. "I held up the wrong pants leg to Simcha." Unmoved, he waited until the child, who kept his balance with difficulty while hanging on my arm, had changed legs. He did not consider me worthy of a glance. I was too stupid to realize the extent to which the Almighty was concerned about which leg His creatures used to step into which pants leg. Or was I too frivolous?

"Do you know what my father says?" asked Avrom a few afternoons later. Mocking, his black eyes pierced mine. Around his mouth appeared a malicious smile. "My father says that you are a *shlechte froi.*" I did my best to appear unmoved, but with the unerring instinct characteristic of children, he spotted me as the weaker one. "He says that you are even worse than Gomer," he added triumphantly. Clapping his hands, he started shouting, "Gomer, Gomer, Gomer!" After hesitating at first, Dov joined in. I fled into the hall, but they came after me, stamping their feet and jeering until Mrs. Kalman appeared in the kitchen doorway.

After work I passed by Café Berkowitz and noticed Mr. Apfelschnitt in the window. I went inside. He was sitting alone at a table, with an empty chessboard in front of him, and he immediately started grumbling. "Just imagine, I've played two games and lost both! And to whom? To Itzik Finkel, it's unbelievable. The man is so dumb. If he falls on his back, he'll break his nose. But he beats me in chess! In no time flat, he beat my knights. Sheer cruelty!"

"He must have beaten more than your knights." I explained that I had no time to join him. I just wanted to know from him who or what Gomer was.

"Gomer? Do you mean the son of Japheth?"

"I don't think so. Wasn't there a woman whose name was Gomer?"

"Certainly, the wife of the prophet Hosea. She was a temple prostitute who participated in pagan fertility rites in honor of Baal. One day Hosea was fed up and chased her out of the house. Gomer personifies all children of Israel who are guilty of idolatry and wantonness: traitors who will be outcast by God, just as a husband casts out his adulterous wife. That is the moral of the book of Hosea. But what do you want with Gomer?"

I shrugged my shoulders.

"That's what happens," he said. "You study to be a philosopher, and before you know it you're an educated pickle. I have never seen you look as sour as you do nowadays. Or is that because of the funeral wreaths that you are making?"

He thumped one of the buttons of the chess clock. "If you ask me, it's high time that you went out dancing with a nice boy."

"On the contrary," I said resolutely, "it's time that I started reading the Bible."

I walked home, dispirited. For some time I had suspected that Mr. Kalman hated me. For Jews like him, who scrupulously obeyed the 613 laws and regulations that they had inherited from the time of Moses, the only joy was in God. Outside of that reigned a void even wilder than the chaos that had preceded Creation. I understood that in the eyes of Mr. Kalman I represented that void and that he felt he should protect his children from it. That was his right. Even the fact that he compared me to an Old Testament slut hardly bothered me. He could tell Avrom and Dov and the whole world that I was a bad woman. As far as I was concerned, he could print it in the paper. But at the thought that he would say the slightest bad thing about me in the presence of Simcha, tears came to my eyes.

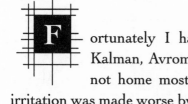ortunately I had little contact with Mr. Kalman, Avrom, and Dov, since they were not home most of the afternoon. But my irritation was made worse by the aggravating concierge.

He was stationed on the ground floor, where he had two rooms. The rest of the floor was taken up by the lobby; the hall; the boiler closet; and a storage area for the vacuum cleaner, floor polisher, and cleaning products. There was also a glass-enclosed porter's lodge, a relic from more prosperous times. But the concierge was almost never in that lodge. Sometimes he would putter around in the hall with a broom. At other times he would block the staircase with a large tool chest.

From the most unexpected corners he would pop up in his grubby coveralls and rush past me as though a vitally important task, which could not be postponed, was awaiting him. When he did sit down to rest, he did so on an old kitchen chair in the lobby, right near the door.

A cigarette butt, seldom lit, always danced in the corner of his mouth. From his coat jangled an enormous chain with keys, which he used to open and lock doors. His dog invariably trudged in his wake. He was a knee-high, shapeless mutt with a groggy expression; he didn't so much carry the name Attila as he was burdened by it. His master directed long monologues to him, fragments of which I caught whenever I was getting the baby carriage ready in the entry. While rubbing his legs he would sigh and say things like, "You're lucky, Attila, you've got healthy legs, but mine are no good. All the blood flows to my feet, the doctor said it himself. Sir, he says, all the blood flows to your feet, you've got to take it easier. That's fine for him to say! A doctor like that sits on his behind. He doesn't even have to stick out his tongue, he lets others do that. He only has to look at it and once in a while write a note for the pharmacy. And for that, he gets paid plenty! But I slave away, climbing upstairs and downstairs from morning till night, for a simple slice of bread."

Attila listened in dull resignation, hanging his head

like someone who knows that contradiction is useless.

"Look at this!" said the concierge, while lighting his stub for the umpteenth time. "These matches today look like flying bombs. The heads whoosh around your ears! This country is going to hell, Attila. Take it from me. The factories are bulging with Algerians and Moroccans. How can camel drivers produce good matches? These people never saw a match at home; back there they still do it with flints!"

The dog was literally talked into the ground. His heavy body sagged onto the worn marble floor where he fell asleep, buried still deeper under his master's flood of words.

"People no longer know what work is. It used to be different. Nowadays they even have Saturday off and vacation at the drop of a hat. And what do they do in between? I'll tell you, Attila. In between they go on strike! It's all because of the Socialists. Everyone is afraid of work. Goof-offs and pains in the neck, that's what they are. The only thing they do is complain. And do they ever complain, Attila. It's complaints that are destroying this country."

I felt sorry for the concierge. He thoroughly disliked his work and himself. But who can be disgusted by himself day in, day out? Only fools and saints. The concierge, who was neither crazy nor holy, had discovered that it was much simpler to reserve his disgust for others. Besides, in this way he rose in his own estimation. As a matter of fact, he rose to such an extent that he wanted to be addressed as "Mr. Caretaker." This title suited him well, since taking care of the house was his only goal. The fact that the house had inhabitants was an unpleasant, incidental circumstance, especially because they were such inferior beings as Jews. If only he could be the guardian of a vacant building at the end of the world! But in such a building a concierge was superfluous. Everything was always against him. Sulking, he moved through the dimly lit bowels of the house, rattling his keys, both guard and prisoner.

In the beginning I used to greet him, but each time, in response, he pulled a rag out of one of his pockets and began rubbing the steel mail slots furiously, mumbling, "Another scratch, Attila. That wasn't there yesterday. Those scratches seem to be falling from the sky here!" He got worked up over fingerprints on the bannister and sand on the doormat. The inhabitants were even guilty of the cracks in the plaster. There was little that did not bother him, but he was offended most by the presence of the baby carriage that I parked in the hallway several times a day in order to carry the twins up or down the stairs. I left the carriage with my heart pounding and with the fervent hope that he wouldn't show up.

But he always jumped into view from somewhere. His constant insults gradually spoiled my work at the Kalmans, in the same way that a chill draft seeping through a small crack can, in the long run, plunge a whole room into icy cold.

One time he was standing in the hall with his back to me. When he heard my footsteps, he made himself so large that I couldn't pass. "This house," he said contemptuously, "is about to collapse! Attila, those damned Jews are turning it into a pigsty. Why should I continue to work my fingers to the bone? If they like living in a stable, that's their business."

With a low voice I growled, "It's a known fact that Jews like to live in stables, since it made baby Jesus, a damned Jew, world famous."

Furious, he turned around. "Did you say something?"

"I wouldn't dare. It probably was your dog. An animal like that sometimes wants to get a word in edgewise."

From that moment on, the concierge and I lived in a constant state of war.


One afternoon, as I was pushing the baby carriage in a crosswalk, the carriage body separated from the frame and fell into the street with Tzivya and Esha inside. To my relief, the girls started screaming at the top of their lungs; they were unharmed. This created a traffic jam. Waiting drivers blew their horns impatiently. The pedestrian light changed several times while I muddled around with the carriage body, which was easy to handle when empty but nearly impossible when weighed down with the two babies.

Later, at the edge of the pond in the park, while Simcha imitated the quacking of the ducks, I racked my memory. Before our departure had I forgotten to attach the carriage body with the metal frame clamps? I was convinced that I had closed them properly. But if I had fastened the carriage body, how in Heaven's name could it have become detached? Was there a question of evil intent? If so, only the concierge could be suspected. I knew that he hated Jews, but could he be so immoral as to tamper with the baby carriage? I immediately rejected that thought as crazy. It wasn't until hours later, upon our return, that my suspicion was rekindled. I had just opened the door when the concierge jumped into view. He was holding a mop handle and was making threatening feints, like a Japanese sword fighter.

"You can't pass," he snarled at me. "It's wet here. You have to wait outside!"

"Please let us through," I said as nicely as possible. "The children are tired."

He lowered the mop stick like a crossing lever and turned around halfway.

"Do you hear that, Attila?" he said, mocking. "They are tired! All afternoon they've been sitting on a bench in the park, and that's made them tired. And now they want to go through my mopped hall with their filthy feet. These damned Jews! They'd like to see the whole city dance to their tune!"

He slammed the door shut in my face.

There we stood, while in the street the busy rush hour traffic had begun. And it was also drizzling.

"You know what?" I said breezily to Simcha. "We'll leave the baby carriage in the street. Then that man doesn't have to be angry at us. If you'll stay with Tzivya, I'll bring Esha upstairs."

With Esha on my arm I tried opening the building door, but it was double-locked. I cursed inwardly and rang the Kalmans' bell. No one answered. Finally I put Esha in the baby carriage next to her sister and started pushing it forward. Bewildered, Simcha walked along with me. When he opened his mouth I feared that he would burst into tears. But no. Looking serious, he said, "Quack." And then, with a big smile, "Quack, quack, quack." I pressed his hand tighter into mine. Back and forth we walked past the house. At first I made repeated attempts to open the door, but I soon stopped that. I didn't want Simcha to know that we were entirely at the mercy of the concierge.

Finally Mrs. Kalman appeared in the doorway. "What's the matter?" she said. "It's getting close to six."

I explained that the concierge had locked us out.

"Oh," she said, "you needn't pay attention to that man."

"But I have to," I answered, "as long as I haven't mastered the art of crawling through the keyhole."

We stepped briskly through the hall, Mrs. Kalman and Simcha in the vanguard and I behind them with the baby carriage. The concierge was nowhere to be seen. But when we arrived at the elevator, he stuck his scrawny head out of the porter's lodge and shouted, "Jewish pigs!"

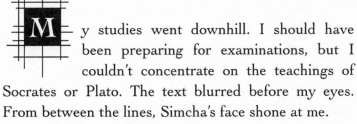 y studies went downhill. I should have been preparing for examinations, but I couldn't concentrate on the teachings of Socrates or Plato. The text blurred before my eyes. From between the lines, Simcha's face shone at me.

Because I wanted to know more about the world in which he lived and from which I was so emphatically excluded, I studied Mosaic law at night. I read parts from the Mishna, the Gemara, and various prayer books. Until early morning I sat bent over the Psalms. I threw myself into the writings of the Prophets as though they were interesting newspaper columns.

And I did all this because of an inexplicable passion

for a toddler who still wet his pants. For him I bought Hasidic music and danced through my room to its compelling rhythm, and for him I did this with so much abandon that I bumped against the table, the closet, and the chairs.

Of course, I also brought home books about the Baal Shem Tov, who had founded the Hasidic movement in the first half of the eighteenth century and who had performed many miracles, according to his followers. When I started delving on a modest scale into the writings of the great master, it quickly became clear to me that Mr. Kalman wasn't all that strict when it came to Hasidic principles. "Let no person imagine that he is better than his fellow creatures," warned the Baal Shem Tov, "just because he serves God with his utmost devotion. For each person serves Him according to the capacity that he has received from the Creator. Even a worm fulfills his task within the limited bounds that God has given him." Was I less than a worm in the eyes of Mr. Kalman? But what was I? A paramecium? A fungus?

I had to choose between two alternatives. Either Mr. Kalman disregarded the lessons of the Baal Shem Tov, in which case, he was a bad Hasid. Or he entrusted the care of his children to a creature who could not even measure up to a worm; in that case, he was a bad father.

One story of the Baal Shem Tov struck me in particular. It was about a powerful king who built a large palace consisting of a maze of rooms. This palace was surrounded by countless walls, with only one entrance hall from which many doors opened. When the construction of the palace was completed, all the important men of the kingdom were invited to visit the king. But when they arrived at the palace, they found the entrance gate bolted shut. Everywhere they saw walls. How would they ever get in? They stood for a long time before the locked gate, until the son of the king appeared. He said, "Don't you see that this whole palace is imaginary? There are no walls here, neither is there a gate nor a door. The void stretches infinitely to all sides. My father, the king, stands before you."

I understood that this king was none other than God. Nevertheless I found the allegory instructive even for unbelievers like me. After all, why couldn't the visitors in the story reach their goal? The way was blocked for them by obstacles so vividly imagined that the walls and the bolted gate seemed real. In the history of knowledge, such examples were legion. Again and again, it seemed that a new interpretation of facts couldn't become possible until imaginary walls and petrified traditions were broken down. The king stood before us in all his majesty. But it had taken us thousands of years to penetrate to one of the outer rooms. With the help of Kepler, Descartes, Newton, and others, we had inched to the next door, but the king wasn't even in view yet.

Every morning in the flower shop I thought about what I had read the night before. I wasn't able to discover in the Jewish religion anything more than a vehicle to guide the children of Israel, who despite many mishaps kept high expectations through world history, *A Streetcar Named Desire* with Moses at the wheel and the Torah in the trunk.

God remained as puzzling as I had always found Him to be. He had nothing in common with people. According to the Torah, He was not born and would never die. How could a God who never had a cold or a stomachache understand anything about human discomforts? And in addition, how could He know our fears, our passions, our hope and our despair? He acted according to a plan that was far beyond our understanding. His name was too holy to be pronounced, and it was forbidden to make images of Him. Photos of God were not in circulation. He was like the Loch Ness monster, which had been seen more than once by befuddled Scotsmen but never by a camera: you had to believe in it in order to see it. Naturally I could study His laws. But these had been written down thousands of years ago in Aramaic shorthand by Jewish mystics who were even further removed from me than the Greeks and the Romans.

When I closed the flower shop door behind me, I saw my father walking. I ran after him and caught him at the corner.

"What are you doing here?" I asked, out of breath.

"I was hoping I'd be accosted by a dishevelled girl with a flowerpot in her arms," he said, pointing to the yellow primrose that I was pressing to my chest.

"From my boss," I told him. "Because I set a record: five funeral wreaths in one morning."

"That many?" he asked.

"Yes, dying is really in style. You don't know what you're missing. A ribbon with the text 'Rest soul, a sweeter destiny awaits you.' Isn't that just the thing for you?"

Together we roamed the southern part of the city, toward the Scheldt River. I wondered what my father was doing near the flower shop. Were the lost suitcases buried somewhere around there? Hanging on his arm, I told him about my work at the Kalmans, their strict mode of life, my weakness for Simcha, and Simcha's weakness for ducks.

When I had finished talking, he said, "It is an ominous sign that the Hasidim, of all people, are considered characteristically Jewish, not only by *goyim* who are happy that they can again point at a Jew on the street, but also by the Jews themselves from a romantic kind of nostalgia. For what do they have this goddamned nostalgia? For the Middle Ages?"

Indignant, I jumped to the defense of the Kalman family.

"You cannot deny that the Hasidim, by holding fast to the old traditions, have saved Judaism from destruction," I said.

My father laughed.

"Old traditions? On the contrary! In the time of the Greeks the Jews behaved as Greeks, in the Arabic Empire as Islamites, in Italy of the Renaissance as Italians, in Holland as Dutchmen. Their synagogues in Moorish Spain cannot be distinguished from mosques. And those in Germany in the Middle Ages were as sober as Protestant churches. Throughout the ages, from Philo in Alexandria to Einstein, from Maimonides to Freud, Jews have influenced their surroundings and were in turn inspired and changed by them. It is precisely to assimilation and communication that Judaism owes its survival. With their sidecurls, their caftans, and their backward ideas, Hasidim are but a caricature of themselves. Hasidism originated in the European ghettos, out of hundreds of years of confinement and humiliation. The Hasidim still walk around in their prison garb from that time. Why? After all, am I still wearing my striped outfit from Sobibor? No Jew in his right mind would nowadays plaster a yellow star on his chest!"

"Aren't you exaggerating just a little?"

"I wish I were! The ghetto walls have been dismantled, but your holy Hasidim are rebuilding them again and again. Don't think that you can change that little boy with whom you walk through the park one iota. It is very unwise even to try it. Should you let a tied-up foal smell the meadow? Are you doing him a favor? Certainly not."

As we talked, we reached the wharf. Bales of cotton were stacked up as high as a wall. The wind pulled on the pale plush that here and there stuck out of the packing. We walked to the river and looked out over the water. Sea gulls floated down like white parachutes to dive for garbage in the waves.

Silently we climbed the stairs to the esplanade. A man was playing *"La vie en rose"* on a hand organ, a pathetic-looking monkey on a chain sitting on his shoulder. My father threw a few coins into a cup at his feet.

In a café overlooking the water he ordered hot

chocolate for me and for himself a cup of coffee, which he left untouched.

"At my elementary school in Berlin, an organ grinder always came and played," he recalled. "Every day he was chased away by the principal, but he always returned. We had bribed him, you see. He was supposed to disrupt the lessons. We took turns paying him our allowances, which we had saved for weeks. That man could sure make a terrific noise on that small organ!"

I laughed, but he shook his head.

"I don't know what's the matter with me," he said softly. "I feel so cheated." He sighed. "Maybe I'm just getting old."

I looked at him. Under his right eye, on the spot where as a child he had been hit by the arrow from a friend's bow, there was a scar, a blue triangle of wild flesh. Under his left eye, from the nostril, there was a diagonal welt from the whip with which an SS officer had called him to order years later. But I knew that postwar surgical weapons had caused most of the scars located on his upper body, making it vaguely resemble a map. With some imagination you could find Stalingrad on it, or Babi Yar, or another place of doom. Pointing to his midriff you could shout: Here Hitler's troops invaded Poland! Each armpit was a mass grave. On his back lonely rails, nowhere crossing each other, ran to macabre terminals.

"What's the matter?" he asked.

"Nothing, I'm just sitting here looking at you."

I looked outside where a freight barge was passing. If the skipper at the helm were my father, I would have grown up with the sound of the motor, the smell of brackish water and tar, and with more wind in my hair than a city child can imagine. I would know the names of harbors instead of concentration camps. The Second World War would be farther away than the horizon. I yawned from boredom at the thought.

"Are you getting enough sleep?" asked my father. "And are you eating well? Your mother worries."

"If she didn't worry about me, she'd find something else to kvetch about. I fill a need." As I was saying this, I regretted it.

"You should know," he said vehemently, "how much I'd like to hear my mother say once more: Wash your hands, button your coat, be careful not to catch cold! I really yearn for that. It would be a true pleasure to let her kvetch my ears off."

He got up angrily and was about to leave without saying goodbye, but he turned around and said in a flat voice, "I love you." That was a habit of his. As far back as I could remember he had spoken those words at every goodbye, no matter how unimportant. He insisted on saying it even when he left the house to run an errand around the corner. Because we could go all up in smoke even before he reached the end of the street. Anything was possible.

**P**assover is a holiday of miracles: the miracle of the ten plagues that struck the Egyptians, the miracle of the angel of death who passed over the houses of the children of Israel, the miracle of the liberation from slavery and the parting of the waters. Like all Jewish holidays, it starts after sundown.

I could well imagine that the sun was eager to set on that day of the year. But the fact that it had risen that morning was to me more miraculous than all of God's miracles put together. Whatever had convinced the sun to climb into the center of the bit of sky above the Jewish quarter of Antwerp? Where did it get the courage?

At the merest crack of dawn the quarter, from which every trace of yeast had been removed, began to ferment like a brewer's vat. In every house windows were pushed wide open. Shrill women's voices pierced the quiet. They expressed themselves in a vocabulary limited to *wake up, get up, hurry up*.

A short while later men and small children fled outside, the sleep still in their eyes. Then all beds were stripped and supplied with spotlessly clean sheets. In prosperous households the blankets had come back from the cleaners the day before. In the part of the quarter inhabited by large and mostly poor families, blankets and spreads were being beaten in the open air. A column of mothers and daughters, aunts and neighbors, stood two by two, snapping them. With the intense gestures of a conductor bringing his orchestra to a thunderous final chord, they beat even the most stubborn bread crumbs out of the bed linens. The street was filled with brightly colored blankets that, in the hands of the women, billowed up and down, like the waves of the Red Sea itself.

The men, if they hadn't sought refuge in the synagogue, were taking care of unfinished business deals. Meanwhile, in alleys between houses and in gutters, groups of children were starting festive bonfires for the ritual burning of yeast. They threw all sorts of things into the flames: not only leftover bits of bread that had been swept up after breakfast, but also cardboard boxes, old newspapers, and sometimes a piece of furniture that had been discarded during the cleaning. The little ones danced around it in a wide circle.

In the afternoon, as I approached the house of the Kalmans, a small fire was crackling there as well, at a safe distance from the front door and the eternally complaining concierge. With an air of importance, Avrom and other big boys were throwing wadded paper and pieces of wood into the flames. Down the street, Dov was jumping around in a circle with a group of friends, singing a Hebrew counting rhyme.

*Who knows one? I know one.*
*One is our God, in Heaven and on Earth.*
*Who knows two? I know two.*
*Two are the tablets of the commandments.*

Further down, at the entrance of the house stood Simcha, his head slightly bowed. I saw his lips move. Coming closer, I heard that he was practicing the questions that he, as youngest son, would have to ask during the Seder. A year ago, Dov had still done it, but now it was Simcha's turn for the first time. *"Mah nishtanah halailah hazeh?"* How is this night different from all other nights? His voice seemed too small for such important words.

He raised his eyes.

"Why do I have to ask the questions if I already know the answers?"

"That's part of the holiday," I said. "You ask the questions and your father answers. Later, when you're a father, you may say the answers."

"I don't want to be a father," he said firmly. "I want to be a duck."

"In the pond in the park?"

He nodded.

"Then I'll come and feed you," I promised while winding one of his red sidecurls around my finger.

"Bread?"

"Yes, I'll bring you bread every day, except on Shabbat. On Shabbat I'll bring you blintzes with sour cream and apricot jam."

He shivered with excitement.

"I can already quack; I still have to learn to swim."

"And fly?" I said.

"Flying is easy." He extended his arms sideways and made flying movements.

I lifted him up. "Don't you want to sing, too?" I asked, pointing to the dancing children.

"No, no, I already know that song. Eleven are the stars in Joseph's dream. Twelve are the tribes of Israel. I have no time for songs, I have to practice the questions." He laid his head against my shoulder. "I hope I don't pee in my pants," he sighed, "I hope I don't pee in my pants." I reassured him and carried him inside, past the concierge who was sitting in the lobby with his dog and who, without looking at us, said, "For all I care, they can burn the whole house down!"

Mrs. Kalman was standing in the middle of the spotless living room. She was even more pale than usual. Tears rolled down her cheeks and dripped onto a stack of plates that she clasped to her chest. For a moment we looked at each other silently, she with her dishes and I with Simcha in my arms. Then she said wearily, "I don't know how long I've been walking around with these plates, from the kitchen to the living room and back."

"Why don't you put them on the table?" I pointed.

She closed her eyes. "Eight days of Passover! What I'd really like to do is lie down on the floor and sleep for eight days."

For a second, it looked as though she were indeed going to do just that. But then she put the plates on the table and dried her face with her apron.

"So much still has to be done before tonight," she said. "And my husband is useless. He doesn't just trade in chocolate, he also thinks in chocolate. Leizer, I said to him yesterday, we can thank the Almighty that Moses didn't trade in chocolate, because then we would never have reached the Holy Land. We would still be slaves in Egypt, and even worse, slaves with rotten teeth." She sighed and prodded me, gently pushing my back. "Please take the girls quickly to the park. I can't have anyone underfoot here."

Tzivya and Esha had already had their bottles. They were awake but lay quietly in their cradle, as though they knew that they shouldn't tax their exhausted mother. As soon as possible I left the house with the girls and with Simcha. But at Pelikaan Street we got stuck in the crowd. Everywhere people were standing or walking, and pandemonium reigned as though a rebellion threatened. I was able to push forward by using the baby carriage as a buffer, but I kept having to wait for Simcha. He was moving on a lower level where he collided with filled shopping bags and flapping coattails.

Stadspark is situated like an equilateral triangle in the center of Antwerp. Although it is visited by many kinds of people, it is known as the "Jewish park." Every afternoon as we entered the park at Quinten Matsijs Avenue, a cluster of Orthodox women stood at the entrance. Mothers with infants in their arms or toddlers clinging to their hands discussed diaper rash, chicken pox, and measles with great animation. Grandmothers admired each other's grandchildren, sang lullabies, or exchanged gossip. Their buzzing had an intimate feeling, as though the whole park were an enlarged living room.

This time, quiet reigned when we reached the park after walking slowly through the crowd. I had expected to find at least a few old folks who had been pushed out of their armchairs by the Passover upheaval. But people had stayed away in droves, as though an announcement had been made that this piece of ground would be struck by a tornado. Cheerfully, Simcha and I walked to the pond. There was very little wind. The weeping willows with their new leaves performed a slow green dance of veils. The rocking motion of the baby carriage had put Tzivya and Esha to sleep. I left them behind on the path and followed Simcha to the edge of the water.

It had taken Simcha weeks to understand that he could trust me. Certainly, I dressed like only the *goyim* did. But my Yiddish, which I had learned from Mr. Apfelschnitt, was the same Yiddish spoken by his mother. And wasn't the concierge as mean to me as he was to the other residents of the house? Therefore I couldn't be too different.

But what really gained me Simcha's affection was our buying half a loaf of bread at the kosher baker in Pelikaan Street every day. I allowed him to feed the bread to the ducks, though he didn't find this easy. With his overdeveloped sense of right and wrong he wanted to give each one an equal portion, but the boldest and fattest ducks were always first in line. In order to reach the last ones, he would turn a few revolutions like a discus thrower. There were times when he would have thrown himself at the ducks along with the bread if I hadn't grabbed him around the waist at the critical moment.

Now, because there was no bread to be bought in the entire quarter, we squatted empty-handed at the edge of the pond. Simcha didn't laugh. Gravely, he observed the diving and splashing. Then he turned to me.

"Does a duck know he's a duck?" he asked.

I shook my head.

"If a duck knew that," I said, "then he'd want to know a lot more. He would no longer splash in the water. He'd come out of the pond and would want to come to school to learn the alphabet."

Simcha nodded. He knew the alphabet. Avrom had taught him to say it perfectly.

*"Aleph, bet, gimel, ∂alet, heh,"* he began, half speaking, half singing.

I put my arm around him.

"Every school would be filled to the rafters with

ducks. Ducks would want to know where New York is, and the North Pole. Ducks would learn Torah, and ducks would pray."

"That's nice," Simcha said happily. He was going to start Yesode Hatorah, the Jewish school, in September. He beamed with joy at the prospect of sharing his desk with one or more ducks.

"Nice?" I said. "When the pond is empty?"

Shocked, he looked at the floating birds.

"A few ducks have to stay here."

"And they're not allowed to find out where New York is? Do they have to stay stupid for the rest of their lives? That will cause terrible trouble."

I stood up and stretched. Hesitating at first, he followed my example.

"Where is New York?" he asked.

"New York is very far away, in America. A duck who knows the alphabet lives there. His name is Donald Duck. He can talk and he drives around in a car. But is he happy? Of course not. Give a duck an inch and he'll want a foot."

We walked to the baby carriage. I lifted him up so that he could see the shining bubble of spit that Tzivya had blown while sleeping.

*"Shayn,"* he said admiringly.

Together we pushed the carriage along the path, in

the direction of the bench where we sat every afternoon. In the silence we heard the squeaking of the wheels and the crunching of the gravel under the soles of our shoes. Simcha began to practice the questions for the Seder aloud again. How is this night different from other nights? Why do we eat unleavened bread and bitter herbs? Why, why, why? I looked at him under my arm, the way he walked next to me in his buttoned-up jacket. How was this child different from other children? Why did I put up with his hateful father, his standoffish mother, his nasty brothers, and a crazy concierge to be in his presence for a few hours a day?

Meanwhile we had reached our bench. I parked the girls and tucked them in tightly. It wasn't until I lifted my head out of the baby carriage that I saw it. With white paint it was plastered on the back of our bench: STINKING JEWS.

"Look," said Simcha, who had already climbed on the bench. He was sitting on his knees and moved his index finger over the letters, from right to left, the way he was used to doing. "They don't have little flags."

I sat down next to him. "No," I said, "because these are not Hebrew letters."

"What does it say?"

"Move your hand so that I can read it."

He held both his arms high up in the air.

"It says: Quack, quack, quack."

His face beamed. I pulled him on my lap, pushed away his sidecurls, and kissed his temples. I poured a flood of endearments over him. "Quack," he said, sighing, "quack."

"Am I interrupting?" someone asked at that moment.

Through my tears I recognized Mr. Apfelschnitt. He introduced himself solemnly to Simcha, felt the back of the bench, and carefully sat down next to us.

"I thought, well, I'll walk to the park, the paint should be dry by now."

"You knew about it?"

"Yes, I left the house right after morning prayer. All these carpet-beaters on the street are driving me crazy. It's as if an army were marching back and forth. Every year I run away from that racket. But when I got here, I couldn't sit anywhere. Everything was still wet and I didn't dare risk my coat."

Everything? I looked down the path. "Do all the benches look like this?"

He nodded. "All of them, complete with stars and planets."

How quiet it was. As though the park were ashamed on its own behalf. And we were part of that shame. Because we had deserved the humiliation? No, because we took it for granted. Instead of getting an ax and using it to hack every painted bench into slivers, we remained seated, Mr. Apfelschnitt and I, with the white letters like a name plate on our back.

He put his hand on my knee for a moment.

"Don't let this spoil your mood. I won't let it either. In my eyes these are primitive cave paintings done by cave men who don't posses language sufficiently to carry on even the simplest dialogue."

On the way back he kept us company. The streets had become quiet, almost as dismally quiet as the park. Mr. Apfelschnitt sang a Polish song to the babies, who smiled at him from under the hood of the carriage. Simcha walked along, quacking softly. In the houses we passed, everyone was making the last preparations for the holiday of holidays. I didn't understand what there was to celebrate.

y landlady rented out practically every square foot of her dilapidated house across from the Royal Museum of Fine Arts. She kept the ground floor for herself, but the other floors were inhabited by all sorts of people. In the moldy stairwell, where the light never worked, it was too dark to recognize anyone, let alone start a conversation.

I rented the attic, which consisted of one room and a small, damp kitchen. I had furnished the room with a bed, a clothes closet, a few chairs, and a table. My books were stacked high against the walls. Through three bay windows I looked out over the large square in front of the museum and at the museum itself, with its bronze triumphal chariots on the corner columns holding up the roof.

The house next to ours had been condemned. The windows facing the street had been boarded up. On the door hung a dented sign with a skull and bones and the warning *danger de mort*. Mice had moved in by the hundreds. They also visited me; I don't know how. They borrowed sugar without asking, and they left droppings behind in the frying pan. In the middle of the night they chased each other above my head. I heard them gnaw on the sheets of polystyrene foam lining the roof. Sometimes I chased them away by standing on a chair and banging the slanted ceiling with a broom a few times. But most of the time I left them alone, thankful that they gave me an excuse for staying awake. Then I would sit down at the table and bend over one of the many books that lay open next to and on top of each other.

In addition to literature about Judaism and Jewish history for which I ransacked used bookstores, I read books about physics and the philosophy of nature, which I brought home from the university library. I was particularly fascinated by astronomy.

As a child I had owned a diorama that showed the night sky. It was a primitive model—just an open shoebox covered with dark blue tissue paper. Against the back wall hung a cardboard crescent moon. It fell down when the glue gave out. The stars stayed in their places. They were holes that I had pricked into the paper with the dull end of my mother's darning needle. In the evening, when I bent under the table lamp with one eye squeezed shut and looked through the peephole in my box, I saw the whole universe in all its glory.

That simple box fascinated me then as much as the facts in my books fascinated me now. Stars turned out to be enormous balls of gas in which hydrogen was transformed into helium with much violence and at extreme heat. Some stars were extinguished, while others had yet to be born. The universe was filled with red, white, and clear blue, young and old, hot and cold stars, which kept a distance from each other through the force of gravity. Without gravity, our whole Milky Way would explode like fireworks. Without gravity, people could not take a step on Earth, not even in the direction of churches, synagogues, or mosques. It wasn't the God of Mr. Apfelschnitt but gravity that governed our life. Still, that knowledge didn't satisfy me. For just as no one could explain who or what God was, the writers of my books were unable to explain gravity. Many questions remained. The universe was not perfect. Sometimes a dying star not only destroyed itself but also swallowed up the surrounding space. At that spot a flaw originated in the cosmos, a hole that was pitch black and quiet and in which time had ceased to exist. In such a black hole were there laws of nature other than ours?

According to the Torah, time and space were an eternal constant, and at Creation God added matter. But now scholars claimed that time and space had not always existed and that both could end in the future. It was also possible that the immeasurable vastness was surrounded by something else, something that was unknown and unimaginable.

When I stood up from the table and walked to the window, I recognized the Little Dipper with the sparkling Pole star at the end of its handle above the museum. Did anything exist outside this cosmos, and if so, what? It could be anything, but surely it wasn't cream of wheat or flowered wallpaper.

I read too much and not enough of anything. I read things that I thought I understood at the time but whose meaning escaped me a few days later. Science seemed a slippery slope on which truth moved continually, remaining out of my reach. According to some physicists, the immense universe had originated from a single molecule. But the smallest particle was a world in itself. In a scientific journal I had seen the enlargement of a submicroscopic part of a virus. It looked like a complicated spaceship surpassing the wildest fantasies of science-fiction films.

Large and small had become interchangeable. When Simcha walked to the park with his hand in mine, his face was a narrow white spot. But in the evening, in my room at the other end of the city, his face took on quite different proportions. It expanded until it covered a whole wall, so that I could not see it in its entirety but had to explore it pore by pore, one eye at a time, from one corner of the mouth to the other, much like a telescope scanning the universe from star to star and from solar system to solar system.

More and more often I would fall asleep over my book. I never slept longer than an hour or two, but I had dreams that I remembered vividly later. For example, I dreamed that my father's lost suitcases were in a black hole in the cosmos. There, in the timeless dark, they lay with their lids open. It turned out that they contained not only the photos of my grandparents but also their dead bodies and that of Aunt Selma, the poison cup still in her hand. I dreamed that as soon as my father had stuck his shovel in the hole, he was swallowed up by the suitcases. And not just he but the whole city: houses, cars, boats on the river, mail carriers, bartenders, prostitutes, and longshoremen, everything and everybody disappeared into my father's suitcases. From the abyss I heard him laughing and calling out, "You see, I always knew that I'd find them!"

At dawn I would be awakened by the tram coming to a screeching halt below in the square. I sat up with a stiff neck. Shivering at the kitchen counter, I subjected myself to the washcloth and toothbrush routine. On the hook next to the potholders hung a small mirror. When I glanced at my reflection there, I understood even less about myself than about the principle of relativity. My mother was right: I was burning up fast. My cheeks were ashen and my eyes were sinking increasingly deeper into their sockets, as though they no longer wanted to have anything to do with me. If I went on living at this speed, I'd be eighty before I'd had the chance to turn twenty-one. Every time I saw my face in that mirror, I resolved to go to sleep on time that evening, preferably in bed, like a normal person. But when I came home after work, the very last thing I wanted to do was sleep.

Every morning I dragged myself to the flower shop where, from sheer exhaustion, I cut most of the carnations too close to the blossom so that they were unusable. "Watch what you're doing!" my boss yelled, incensed. But I had difficulty keeping my eyes half open.

Then, gradually, I got over my fatigue. When afternoon finally arrived, my blood started rushing faster. The thought of seeing Simcha again set my legs in motion. Relieved, I pulled the shop door shut behind me. I crossed the square, bought two ounces of green olives in the Spanish store in Graaf van Egmont Street, and went home. I ate those olives with a piece of brown bread while once again leafing through one of my books. Then I threw the chewed pits into a water jug that my landlady had given me and that stood at a distance on the floor. An hour later I walked with renewed energy to the Kalmans' house.

Antwerp had skipped spring to plunge head over heels into summer. And such a summer! The sky was as smooth as a tightly stretched sail. The existence of clouds, even the smallest, disappeared from our memory. Not a drop of rain fell, and the temperature kept rising. In the afternoon, Simcha and I walked hand in hand through the park, without coats and with the sun on our faces. For several weeks we had observed the ducks nesting from a distance, and now the pond was suddenly teeming with ducklings in and around it. Enchanted, Simcha watched as the yellow, brown, and spotted balls of down tumbled into the water, clambered back onto the edge, and, ten or more at a time, rolled under the body of the mother duck. What most surprised him was that they stayed afloat so easily.

"When I become a duck, I want to be a boy duck," he said emphatically. "Because I'm a boy."

*"Mazel tov,"* I said, laughing, "because then you get a beautiful green head. Only the males have such a head. The females stay brown."

"Why do they stay brown?"

"Because that makes them less conspicuous when they're hatching their eggs in the bushes. Look, they are the color of sand and twigs."

He reflected. "Don't I get a red head? I've got red hair."

"I forgot all about that! Perhaps you'll be the only red duck in Antwerp! A red duck with red sidecurls wearing a black hat. Then people will ask each other, Have you seen that red duck swimming in the pond, that duck with a hat? And then they'll say: *Gut yomtov,* Mr. Duck, how are you today?"

Simcha nodded. "I'd like a hat but no pants. Without pants I can't pee in them."

I pulled him onto my lap and stroked his nose with my index finger. "When you're a duck," I whispered, "you can pee all you want. And no one will see it in all that water."

**M**y contact with fellow students was limited to lectures, which I seldom attended. At the start of the school year, when I still showed up with some regularity, I was approached by a girl named Sophie. I couldn't get rid of Sophie. She sat down next to me in the lecture halls and in the cafeteria, where she did her utmost to start a conversation. Since she left me no other choice, I began to feel a vague liking for her.

At any rate she was more interesting than most of the other students. They complained loudly when a professor assigned us a book to read, or even worse, two books. Sophie read much and enjoyed it. And she had a passion: Friedrich Nietzsche. She couldn't stop talking about him. "We must have the courage to let go of all inhibitions and to follow our instincts. We must indulge our vital passions without constraint. Down with mediocrity and slave mentality!" *Also sprach* Sophie.

"Nietzsche's ideas are suitable for bulls," I said. "But they are disastrous in a china shop."

"Nonsense. He's a champion of the free development of man. He wipes the floor with moralizers who heap guilt and shame upon us. According to Nietzsche, we aren't truly free until we're no longer ashamed of ourselves!"

"True, but the world's population consists mostly of the scum of the earth who have all the reasons in the world to be ashamed. Sons of bitches who have latched on to Nietzsche's philosophy to justify common crimes."

"Can he help that? That's exactly what he feared so much and what he warned about more than once. He wanted to prevent the misuse of his ideas."

"That fear was well-founded. Very little has been written that lends itself so well to misuse."

"That proves only that he was far ahead of his time."

"Far ahead? Exactly thirty-three years after his death the Neanderthals came to power in Germany and fulfilled his boldest dreams."

Sophie's eyes shot fire. "Hitler fulfilled only his

own dreams! He didn't correspond at all to Nietzsche's image of the aristocratic ruler."

"But he did use all the ideas outlined by Nietzsche: violence, disdain for the weak, ruthlessness, and so forth."

"True, but you can't blame Nietzsche for that. At the most you can say that Nietzsche has written a cookbook that fell into the hands of the wrong chef."

Impatiently I brushed aside her argument. "There are no chefs who can prepare something that tastes good or is even palatable with such ingredients. They turn on the gas and get no further. We've seen that, haven't we? Nietzsche's ideas are good for philosophers. But they're unsuitable for people."

"Slaves are the only ones for whom Nietzsche's ideas are unsuitable. You are simply too much of a coward to free yourself."

"Certainly, if it's at the expense of others."

Sophie shrugged her shoulders. "To grow you have to put your own interest first. Everyone is selfish. Whoever doesn't stand up for himself will be crushed."

"You act as though it is a question of being crushed or of crushing others. As though there isn't an ocean of possibilities between those two. Naturally I'm selfish, but I'm not particularly proud of that characteristic. Nietzsche makes it a necessity."

"What's wrong with that?"

"If you don't understand that, I can't explain it to you. Either you are ethical or you aren't. Nietzsche said that himself. Incidentally, Nietzsche said other things. He said that women are stupid and superficial beings. Whenever women instead of men were plagued by vital passions, Nietzsche called them undisciplined and frivolous. He believed that at such times they should be ignored or swept aside, preferably with a whip."

She dismissed my objections. "If you're super-critical, nothing will remain of any philosophy!"

Sophie, who was tall and blond and more beautiful than Marilyn Monroe, didn't have to fear any whip. Men wanted to do her anything but harm. Every Saturday evening she went out with another boy and later she would tell me wild tales. With one of them she had made love on the roof of an old car in a drafty parking garage, and her underwear had blown away. With another she had spent the night in a warehouse at the port, just outside of the reach of barking, bloodthirsty watchdogs. She claimed that she wanted to live dangerously, like Mussolini. It seemed evident to me that the living Mussolini enchanted her more than the dead one who had been strung up upside down like a pig on a meat hook.

One evening I went with her to a departmental faculty party after we had both passed our examinations. We had agreed to meet in front of Central Station, but an hour earlier, she rang my doorbell to pick me up. First, she lay down on my bed, then she paced up and down the room, lifting books from stacks at random. *"Zur Kabbala und Ihrer Symbolik,"* she read aloud. "Albert Einstein, *The World As I See It.*" She pointed to a poster on the wall. "He's even hanging over your bed. What is it between you and Einstein?"

"I love his mustache," I said, laughing. "But you probably like Nietzsche's mustache better." It would have been better not to have said that because while we were descending the stairs in the dark she began to explain why I couldn't embrace Nietzsche's philosophy. She concluded that my Christian background stood in my way.

"That doesn't seem very likely," I snapped, "especially since I'm Jewish." I slammed the front door behind us. It suddenly dawned on me that I'd had it with Sophie's nonsense, and I wasn't planning to be patient anymore.

"I thought that you were German," she said, "because of your last name."

"My parents are Jews. My father did grow up in

Berlin, but in nineteen thirty-five he didn't find it very *gemütlich* anymore, and he fled to Brussels."

"You never told me that. Then Chaya is a Jewish name?"

I nodded. "It means 'she lives.' I think that my parents, who after the war were more dead than alive, named me that to bet on a sure thing. Therefore, I'd like to talk about something other than *Übermenschen* tonight. Because those *Übermenschen* of yours can exist only by the grace of *Untermenschen*."

We walked side by side silently.

After a while, Sophie said, "My father has always worked for the state police. That's why we couldn't rent an apartment in a house where Jews lived. It was forbidden. I never had any contact with Jews. I wouldn't have dared. My mother said that I shouldn't play with Jewish children because I'd get warts."

She looked at me out of the corner of her eye. "Your father doesn't have a beard and those corkscrew curls, does he?"

I shook my head.

"That's how Jews bring a lot of misery on themselves," she added immediately. "They don't want to fit in."

"You think so?" I said. "My father fitted in so damned well that he ate bratwurst. Even his pajama pants were ironed. He could pronounce words like *Oberlandesgerichtspräsident* and *genossenschaftliche Gemeinschaftarbeit* without even taking a breath. Still he was identified as an enemy of the people. That's what it was called then. Now it has a different name."

"Perhaps," said Sophie, "but in Antwerp it's the fault of the Jews themselves that people look down on them."

"There's a story about Emperor Hadrian," I said. "One day, on the street, he was passed by a Jew who greeted him. 'Peace be with you,' said the Jew. Furious, the emperor screamed, 'Who does that Jew think he is? He greets me as though I were his equal! Put him to death!' After this, another Jew came by who had seen what had happened to the first Jew. Cautiously, without greeting, he walked around the emperor. 'How dare he?' screamed Hadrian. 'He passes me, the ruler of a mighty empire, as though I were a dog. Kill him immediately!' The emperor's advisors didn't understand this. 'You had the first Jew killed because he greeted you,' they said, 'and the second one because he failed to greet you. That doesn't seem logical.' Emperor Hadrian answered, 'You don't have to tell me why I should kill Jews. I can always find a pretext.' *Se non è vero, è bene trovato.*"

Not until the next street did Sophie open her mouth again.

"I didn't know that you were Jewish," she said, embarrassed. "You don't look it at all."

"Is that meant as a compliment?"

She squeezed my arm amicably.

"I've got nothing against you," she said. " I detest only those Jews who hang around near Central Station. They stick together, wearing those ridiculous hats, and they talk of nothing but money all day long."

"How can you know that they talk about money if you've never had contact with them?"

"Not contact, no, but I still see them. It's impossible not to see them! You're practically crushed underfoot by them in Pelikaan Street. They march three or four abreast and don't move aside, so that you have to step off the sidewalk to be able to pass."

"I'm never bothered by that," I said. "Every day I go to work through the Jewish quarter."

"Of course it doesn't bother you." Sophie laughed. "You're Jewish yourself. They do it only to us."

"And a minute ago you claimed that I don't look Jewish at all!"

"Jews recognize each other," she said in a tone that made any further discussion pointless.

I couldn't stand it longer than an hour at the party. Sophie had withdrawn nervously to the dance floor. Standing on the side, my anger increased as I emptied glass after glass of fruit juice at a furious speed. Was it true that she had never lived under one roof with Jews and had not been allowed to play with Jewish children? Had she truly had a *judenrein* upbringing? Once more I spotted her in the dancing crowd. She threw a panicky glance in my direction.

Had she remembered her mother's warning and was she now afraid that she would get covered with warts? I wished her the warts of at least twenty large wart hogs. Light as a feather, I walked back to my attic and to my books.

On one of my days off, I took a bus to Temse where the Scheldt is loveliest. Rivers conform to their surroundings. In the city they are in a hurry. Foaming and wild, they dash against the quay. But as soon as they reach the countryside, they slow down. Calmly they slosh against green banks, stared at by cud-chewing cows and an occasional farmer.

In Temse, a warm and gusting wind had turned the village into a large tumble-dryer. I took the ferry to the other bank and went to sit at the water's edge. I looked at the sunlight darting from wave to lazy wave. The distant bleating of sheep came closer and then disappeared.

I was tired. That's what happens when you sit reading for nights on end. What did I hope to gain by it? The doubt about God's existence with which I had started my exploration of the Torah had given way to doubt of my doubt. Even Albert Einstein seems to have held the opinion that the cosmos can't be a random coincidence and that there must be an underlying plan. According to him, a superior intelligence, which can barely be grasped by people, reveals itself in the universe. Once in a while it happens that some people, with their insignificant understanding, recognize the handiwork of God in one small detail or another, but they are unable to understand the whole. And this was stated by, of all people, a man who had outsmarted God. Like a modern Moses, he had added a commandment to the Torah: matter and energy are interchangeable. This commandment, which makes it possible for mortals to change matter and to control it, had humiliated, if not emasculated, divine authority. How long could the Eternal remain who He was, now that man was in the process of unraveling the secrets of His creation? And how could Einstein believe in the power of anything but mindless nature?

I sat up, pulled off my shoes, and let my feet dangle in the water up to my ankles. I took a pencil and writing pad out of my bag.

"Dear Albert Einstein," I wrote. I stuck the tip of the pencil in my mouth and glanced at my feet, which seemed to lead a life of their own under water and threatened to swim away from me.

"Too bad that you're dead," I continued. "If you were still alive you'd be able to sit on the grass with me. That is, if you'd want to, which isn't very likely. I never got better than a seven in physics. That it wasn't a six was due to the fact that Mr. Brongers liked me. He wanted to dance with me at every school party, and when he did, he never lifted his feet, probably to demonstrate the force of gravity.

"My letter has nothing to do with physics. I don't know your studies about quanta, the photo-electric effect, and other discoveries, perhaps because I don't need them for anything. In the morning I make funeral wreaths in a flower shop in Tol Street, and in the afternoon I work as a nanny. In those occupations I can get along very well without the theory of relativity.

"I've read your biographies, first the one by Seelig and then the one by Snow. In them you are depicted as a brilliant eccentric. This is also how everyone knows you from the photos. In baggy pants and a wrinkled jacket, like a child who has been allowed to dress himself for the first time. And with that mustache in which any bird would like to make a nest.

"For the first time I'm now reading a book that wasn't written about you but by you. I found a used copy of the English translation of *Mein Weltbild* in a store on the Vlasmarkt. Just my luck: pages 26 and 27 are completely stuck together. There's a slice of cheese between them that has fused with the paper, and I can't separate them. Not even holding the pages over the steam of my teakettle works. In this au gratin book, you claim that nothing in the cosmos has been left to chance. You write that God doesn't roll dice.

"First I thought that you were speaking figuratively, but you really seem to mean God when you say God. I'm disappointed in you. You make a fundamental discovery and then you let God have all the credit. Have you taken into account that God might understand as little about the perihelion movement of Mercury as I do? It's not unthinkable that God would get a big fat failing grade in physics from Mr. Brongers. I would like to discuss that with you some time.

"According to Mr. Apfelschnitt, one of my father's friends, atheism has caused nothing but misery. He says that something as horrible as Auschwitz could become possible only because people dropped God and the Bible like a brick. But the Bible isn't exactly nonviolent. And the problem seems to be that people never really abandoned God but tried to find a replacement for Him in Stalin or Hitler. Your world view of an organized cosmos with an infallible being that operates the controls puts them in the right. I wonder whether God is as misplaced in theoretical physics as a slice of cheese is in a book."

At that moment the paper was spattered by a couple of big waves. A heavily loaded ship, called *Utopia*, chugged past. On board stood a woman with sunburned arms who was washing the cabin windows. I watched her until she became one with the ship and the ship became one with the water. Then I laid the soaked notebook in the grass and stretched out next to it. Blinded by the dazzling void of the sky, I closed my eyes.

Late in the afternoon I woke up from a deep sleep. The air was scorching dry. My cheeks were burning. When I finally reached the bus stop in the village, I had to rest by leaning against the glowing-hot brick front of the nearest house.

The ride back to Antwerp seemed to take hours. At one point, at a curve in the road, we passed a field in which at least a hundred children were standing. Each one was holding a cheap badminton racket strung with bright green plastic. But something was wrong with their game. They weren't really playing at all. None of them had a shuttlecock or had contact with one another. Pell-mell, their backs to one another, they stood in the grass and waved their rackets around in slow motion. Their large pale heads swayed in rhythm.

"Down's syndrome children," a passenger in front of me whispered to her neighbor.

Several kilometers later I still saw the children as they had been standing in that bone-dry field under the broiling sun. They were many, but each one was all alone in the world. With their green strung rackets they scooped the air and threw it over their shoulders. Did they know what they were doing? Probably not. Their movements were aimless. It was the serious dedication with which they made their movements that gave them meaning. And this dedication filled me with a profound happiness. It was as if these children had let me in on one of the most important secrets of life.

**M**r. Apfelschnitt came down with a stubborn flu from which he recovered very slowly. I went to see him, bringing a bunch of anemones. In my honor he got out of bed. In his charcoal gray robe he looked as solid as he did in his usual dark suit. But his neck looked thin sticking out of the collar, and his cheeks were sunken.

Grumbling, he laid my bouquet outside his field of vision.

"You give me no pleasure with flowers. From the moment that their stems are cut, they begin to die. I have never understood what civilized people like about looking at rotting flowers in a vase. My own deterioration is sufficient for me."

He had a coughing fit. It was stuffy in the room. The windows and balcony doors were closed tight. I offered to open them, but he made a gesture not to do that. "The street noise bothers me. Perhaps because I don't participate in it."

He sank further into his armchair and, sighing, closed his eyes. He said that it was sweet of me to bring flowers to an old man but that it was against Jewish law. Didn't I know that plants should not be destroyed if in doing so we harmed any animal no matter how insignificant? And weren't flowers a source of food for honeybees, bumblebees, and other insects? Mr. Apfelschnitt felt a great respect for all that was alive. Because the Talmud taught that unnecessary pain to animals should be prevented, he ate neither meat nor fat. He did drink milk, but never without saying beforehand, "May the cow which has given this milk lead a long life."

Silently I gazed at the designs on the carpet. I knew the pattern by heart. Then I looked at the globe, which stood on the writing table and which I had spun on its axis for many years. This had worn the surface. The continents and oceans had faded. From a distance I looked for the tropic of Cancer and the tropic of Capricorn. I found the dotted shipping routes without difficulty: New York–Bremerhaven; Southampton–Capetown. These names had once fascinated me. I remembered when a tiny spider had fallen from my hair and landed in Xianphang in China. It had raced quick as a flash to Greenland and then to all points of the compass. Mr. Apfelschnitt had applauded and exclaimed, "The Marco Polo of spiders!" He and I also traveled quite a lot. Sometimes we crossed the equator at least twenty times and were keelhauled every time. Those were the days!

Now we sat together, down in the dumps. "Throw everything open anyway," he said, wheezing. He dabbed his forehead with a handkerchief. The doors of the balcony squeaked. Hot air mixed with exhaust hit me in the face. "This doesn't help much," I said. "You should buy a fan."

He nodded. "When the Messiah comes." He always said that when he wanted to postpone something indefinitely.

I turned around. "Do you really think that the Messiah will come?"

He nodded and said a well-known prayer.

"Even when he delays, I believe; despite everything. Despite everything, I expect him every day."

"So he could be at the door any moment? In that case, you should have shaved."

"For the time being, he has been delayed."

"And you still expect him?"

"I expect him, against my better judgment. It doesn't matter much if and when he comes; what matters is that we yearn for him." He chuckled. "Do you know the joke about the poor Jews in Warsaw who are exchanging one hovel for another? All day long they're busy moving their ramshackle furniture. In the evening they're finally installed with their stuff in the umpteenth leaky attic. Their nine children are lying on straw mattresses strewn among the clutter. Down in the street a man is running and shouting with joy: 'The Messiah has come, the Messiah has come!' The wife heaves a big sigh and says, 'That's all I need!'"

Mr. Apfelschnitt was a follower of the ideas of Isaac Luria, a sixteenth-century cabalist from Safed. Luria taught that in the beginning everything was filled with divine infinity. To create the world, God had to abolish His own infinity. He withdrew into Himself and made space for matter. This is how the cosmos, the Earth, and man came into being. And this is also how evil came into being. From His exile, God let His light shine, but at a catastrophic moment the enormous power of this light shattered all the spheres, and light became dispersed into space. With the dispersion of the divine light began the Diaspora of the Jews, whose task it was to gather the stray sparks and in that way restore the cosmos to its former perfection. According to Luria, this restoration could be expedited by study of the Torah and obedience to divine commands.

Luria's new outlook had changed life for Jews all over the world. They were no longer required to wait idly for their redemption by the Messiah. Each individual Jew could speed up redemption by praying, fasting, and loving his neighbor as himself. Formerly, Jews had explained their dispersion over the Earth as an ordeal sent by God that they had to undergo passively. Under the influence of Luria, the Diaspora became a positive force, the condition for, as well as the introduction to, *Olam Ha-ba*, the World to Come. The person of the Messiah became less important. The crucial thing was to prepare his way. Mr. Apfelschnitt did this to the best of his ability. I knew no one who was able to unite obedience to God and love for humanity as harmoniously as he. This mild attitude probably resulted not only from his character, but also from his habit of drinking vodka from morning till night. At breakfast he invariably ate two slices of buttered brown bread sprinkled with salt, which he washed down with two glasses of Stolichnaya. He said that it activated the stomach juices. At night this bottle would be three quarters empty. He was never drunk, but I still had the impression that the liquid didn't so much improve his digestion as it softened his judgment of the world.

Not even the flu stopped Mr. Apfelschnitt from drinking. He declined as ridiculous my offer to squeeze lemons for him. After he had poured the umpteenth glass of vodka down his throat, sweat ran over his forehead.

"What heat!" he sighed. "The last time I experienced such heat was in nineteen forty-six. Or was it nineteen forty-seven? I was waiting for a visa in a German camp for displaced persons."

"How long did you stay there?"

"A little over three years. The camp was under control of the British. It had been better under the Americans. We had to perform hard labor: clear out rubble, help with rebuilding. Our hearts weren't in it. We worked alongside German civilians and with *Volksdeutschen* who had been driven out of Czechoslovakia and Hungary and who were also being held in the camp. One evening the British military police came and chased hundreds of us out of our houses to make room for these *Volksdeutschen*. We were dumped into overcrowded barracks at the other side of the grounds. That was against the rules, since the United States had granted special status to Jews and to others who had been persecuted during the war. Because we were in such bad shape, we received some extra food and the best possible housing. But now we had to yield our beds to people who had not only collaborated with the Third Reich but most of whom had also zealously butchered Jews."

"Humiliating."

"Not only that. The *Volksdeutschen* themselves were terribly embittered. They were outraged that they had been sent away from the homelands they had betrayed and in addition had to leave behind their possessions. They blamed the Jews for their own misfortunes as well as for knowingly plunging Europe into war. Therefore we not only had to look on powerlessly as they took possession of our living quarters, but we also had to endure their blazing hatred."

"Did the British do anything about that?"

"The British didn't exactly express favorable opinions about Jews. General Morgan, the chief of all refugee camps in Germany, declared to journalists that the Jews didn't look like victims of any persecution at all. On the contrary, they were in the best of health and there was a danger that they would become a world power. This was announced by Mr. Morgan one week before my wife died of exhaustion and malnourishment."

He blinked his eyes. "A world power!" he said hoarsely. "The report appeared in the *New York Times*. The headline above it mentioned a Jewish conspiracy. One of us had managed to get hold of a copy. We couldn't believe our eyes. It was January nineteen forty-six, barely a year after the murder of millions of Jews had shocked the West. That shock didn't last very long."

He drank another glass of vodka. "Not in Auschwitz, but in a refugee camp did the truth finally dawn on me. In Auschwitz I had no hope, simply because the Nazis left us no hope. But I expected some decency from the so-called civilized world." He raised his voice. "Not much decency," he said with emphasis, "since I had learned to be satisfied with very little. I wanted a passport. And the freedom to live somewhere. A room by myself with a door that I could close and a window through which I could see the sky. But it was asking too much. For years they left us sitting there. They had no time to take a passport out of a drawer. Just as before the war, they were too busy squabbling about which country would admit Jews and how many. Belgium accepted eight thousand. That's a lot if you think that a large country like Canada admitted sixteen thousand and France no more than two thousand."

"Do you think that someone like Morgan really believed in a Jewish conspiracy?" I asked.

"Why not? Before, people were convinced that we could cause the sun to darken and destroy their harvest with hail. People believed the craziest things: that Jews had horns and a tail; that Jewish men menstruated. Nowadays, when astronauts walk around on the moon, you can no longer tell people such nonsense. No one believes any longer that we desecrate the Eucharist or butcher Christian children at Easter. Hatred of Jews has kept up with the times. Nowadays we no longer poison the well at the local market place; instead we poison the whole world. Behind the scenes we hatch plots against humanity. Who started the French Revolution? The Jews, your Majesty. Who caused Germany to lose the first World War and made them start the second one? The Jews, Herr Reichskanzler. Hatred has remained the same, but the explanation for it has been adapted to modern needs. In fact, every anti-Semite is straight from the Middle Ages."

He sneezed a few times and blew his nose at length.

"I used to be just like you," he said. "People like General Morgan have turned me into a Jew. In the ghetto of Krakow I didn't belong; even in Auschwitz I felt like an outsider. But the longer a blind man lives, the more he sees. When I arrived in Antwerp, I bought myself a prayer shawl and *tefillin*. I attached a *mezuzah* to my doorpost and went to a synagogue."

"From one day to the next?"

He nodded. "Perhaps I jumped from the frying pan into the fire. I don't care." He had another coughing fit and gasped for breath, leaning forward in his chair. I thumped him on the back as though he were a dog, an old sick dog. When he finally caught his breath again, I led him to his bedroom where he lay down on his bed, still wearing his slippers. Before he fell asleep he insisted that I take the anemones with me. "For every flower that is picked, a shiver goes through the Earth," he murmured.

he Kalman children possessed nothing that could be called a toy. In the bedroom shared by Avrom, Dov, and Simcha, there was a small closet that consisted of two shelves with a curtain in front. It contained a puzzle with a picture of Moses descending the mountain with the stone tablets of the law, a dreidel, and a number of simple prayer books. There were also a few wooden rattles of the kind that children use to make an infernal racket whenever the name of the Jew-hater Haman is mentioned during the reading of the scroll of Esther at the festival of Purim. In the whole apartment there was no game of dominoes, no ball, not even a crayon to be found.

Once in a while Avrom would read to his brothers from a grubby book called *Lessons for Youth*. In this book, Jewish precepts were set forth in a language that was anything but youthful.

"The celebration of the Shabbat consists not simply in the avoidance of prohibited labor," he read with an air of importance. "In fact, the entire manner in which we spend this holy day must be in accordance with its elevated meaning. In going, our step should be soft and quiet. No remembrance of our daily worries may overshadow our speaking and thinking. In addition, we should not set foot outside the area in which our living quarters are situated, and this means an area not farther than two thousand Jewish ells to all four sides."

"What are Jewish ells?" Dov wanted to know.

Avrom raised his arm.

"From here," he said pointing to his elbow, "to the tip of your index finger. Two thousand times that distance. That's how far you may go from home."

"How can you measure that if it's forbidden to do work on the Shabbat?" asked Dov.

"You just do it on another day," said Avrom.

Dov dropped to the floor and crawled around on

his knees while placing one arm in front of the other.

"Do you have to crawl like this on the sidewalk? And what if you have to cross the street? And what if you lose count?"

"You don't lose count," said Avrom offended. "And you have to count only once. For example, you can count the ells between our house and the railroad station. If it is two thousand, then you know that you can never go past the station."

"And if you want to go in the other direction?"

Sighing, Avrom shrugged his shoulders and continued leafing through the book.

"Is there anything about ducks?" Simcha asked, curious.

"No," answered Avrom, "but it does say that children are not allowed to pee in their pants. Not on Shabbat and not on other days. Children who pee in their pants are taken away to *gehinnom* by evil spirits."

The next afternoon, when I was alone with Simcha, I took the book from the shelf. Upon seeing it, he dived fearfully under the foot of his bed. I leafed through it furiously.

"Hmm," I said. "Nowhere do I see anything about children who pee in their pants or about evil spirits. Nowhere. But I do see something about ducks."

Above the edge of the bed his tearstained face appeared. He rubbed his eyes. "I knew it," he said in a small, trembling voice while he came to sit beside me.

"Regarding ducks," I said solemnly, moving my index finger along the lines. "On the first day, God created light and darkness. On the second, third, and fourth days He created the heavens, water, land, and other difficult things. Then the fifth day dawned. 'Well,' said God, 'now I'd like to create something nice. Ducks, for example.' He started work immediately, but it wasn't as easy as He had thought. The first duck turned out to be an elephant instead of a duck. The next one became a crocodile. 'They are fine,' said God, 'but they are not ducks, you can see that easily.' He created rabbits and kangaroos and calico cats. Then He found a handful of colored feathers in His pants pocket. 'Wait,' He said, 'if I'm not mistaken I have some duck bills somewhere.' He created a lot of ducks and put yellow legs under them. 'They turned out so well!' exclaimed God. 'And they quack so nicely. I've already got so many angels flying around in Heaven, otherwise I'd take ducks.'"

"And then?" asked Simcha.

I turned the page and frowned.

"Then it was evening and it was the sixth day. On that day God created people. He blessed them and said,

'Be fruitful, become numerous, don't trip over the creatures that crawl on the Earth, live long and happily. And if you have leftover bread, give it to the ducks, because I love them more than anything else under the sun.' "

"Me too," said Simcha, and he stuck his thumb in his mouth contentedly.

With the money I earned that week, I bought a wooden duck on wheels in a toy store. It was yellow with a bright red bill and it had a stick for pushing.

"He is much too big for that!" said Mrs. Kalman, shaking her head when Simcha unwrapped his present. But she didn't protest when he strolled with it through all the rooms, the hall, and the kitchen. He called the animal Tchotchke, a Yiddish word meaning "little toy." Tchotchke's only defect was that he couldn't quack. To educate Tchotchke, we had to visit the ducks in the pond. In the beginning, he tended to get stuck between the wheels of the baby carriage, but soon Simcha knew how to steer his rolling duck skillfully.

Only Mr. Kalman objected, but not very insistently, to Tchotchke's presence in the house.

"What can he learn from that?" he complained to his wife, so that I could hear him. He was wrong. From the moment of Tchotchke's appearance in the Kalman home, Simcha was toilet-trained.

**I** n discussion groups at the university, arguments flared not only about the urgently needed student participation in university policies but also about such subjects as the oppression of Antwerp longshoremen, American imperialism in Vietnam, the colonels' government in Greece, the Franco regime in Spain, Portuguese aggression in the African colonies, and the destructiveness of capitalism in general. For all these complicated issues there was one simple solution: revolution. This was demonstrated by a film about sugar production in Cuba where, ever since the departure of the dictator Battista and the arrival of Fidel Castro, people did their work singing.

Occasionally I attended these evening meetings. I wanted to believe that equality among people was possible. But the communist utopia of Marx seemed as unreachable as the messianic paradise prophesied by Isaiah. I was more likely to believe that the lion would lie down with the lamb and the panther with the kid, than that there would come a day when people would no longer kill each other. Communists had done little to convince me of their good intentions. Recently, Russian tanks had violently turned the Prague spring into a Siberian winter. My revolutionary fellow students lost no sleep over this. If asked, some of them hesitatingly admitted that the Soviet Union had chosen a rather unfortunate direction in this matter, but they considered the subject closed, a holdover from Stalin. At any rate, they assured me, Marx's ideas had not caused the invasion. They called me simple and said that I had no right to talk about such matters as long as I had not immersed myself in the totality of socialist ideas.

So I started at the source by reading essays by Buonarroti and Fourier. I was shocked to discover that many nineteenth-century French socialists called Jews all sorts of names. Proudhon thought that Jews were the greatest enemies of humanity. According to him, Jews should be exterminated or sent to the plains of Asia. Sorel, another socialist pioneer, argued for a violent struggle of the working class against Jewish capitalism.

But I was most disappointed by Marx, who seemed to have gone along with the fashion of the time. I didn't understand how the grandson of a rabbi could have let such obvious lies about Jews flow from his pen. He characterized them as selfish exploiters who worshiped no other god but money. Following the example of the French socialists, he spoke of "the Jew" as if only one existed: a sly and unreliable being who embodied all the bad characteristics of those who persecuted him with deadly hate.

I read as though possessed, and pushed myself to the limit. Often, even though it was well past midnight, I had to force myself to lie in bed. I seldom slept more than three hours and never without interruption. I would wake in a sweat from nightmares in which fire and brimstone fell from the heavens. Sometimes I was so frightened that I shot out of bed and pressed myself against the wall, but even in my half-sleep, the dream continued. Once I saw the museum burning. Flames leaked from the windows and threatened to jump over to my attic at any moment. Moaning, I put on my coat, grabbed a stack of books from the table, and fled. It wasn't until I had pulled the attic door closed behind me that I came to. Dazed, I looked at the books in my arms. The depth of the stairwell made me dizzy. I went back into my room sheepishly and didn't dare close an eye for the rest of the night.

For weeks I was tormented by fearful dreams in which fire always played a role, although the dreams differed otherwise. It was as if my unconscious were determined to find the most effective way to scare me to death while I slept. The way was obvious. It was easy to find my weak spot. Simcha began to appear in a dream that recurred nightly. The scenario was simple. We were sitting next to each other on our bench in the park. Suddenly, without apparent cause, he started to burn. Not burn but smolder. It was a smoldering on the outside, caused by sparks so deep inside him that I could not extinguish them. I tried, but it seemed as if an invisible breath kept fanning the fire. Simcha didn't scream. He didn't panic. Quacking sadly, he let himself be consumed by the fire. After the dream, I kept hearing this quacking. Petrified, I lay in bed on my back, my face bathed in tears.

At the flower shop, carnations slipped from my fingers. Daylight hurt my eyes. While standing over a ribbon with the words *Sleep gently, dear deceased*, I nodded off. But most of the time I managed to stay awake by thinking with all my might of my mother and the cart that she had pulled through Auschwitz. I imagined that an SS officer was standing right behind me and that he would shoot me in the back at the slightest provocation. Then I would begin to work feverishly.

Mr. Apfelschnitt was back on his feet again, but the illness had left its mark. He looked tired. His pants were too large and were held up by suspenders, which violated his dignity. He listened to the story of my recurring nightmare with a frown that gradually deepened. "Whoever runs from fire falls into water," he finally said.

"I'm not expecting an explanation," I replied abruptly. "Dreams are a collection of impressions and memories. You can go in any direction with them."

He shook his head vehemently. "According to the old cabalists, there are no dreams without meaning. While man is asleep, his soul leaves his body and rises to great heights. There, each soul has a message whispered to it by the angel Gabriel who rules over the realm of dreams. Such messages are revealed to man in the form of dreams. Rabbi Simeon even said that nothing happens on Earth unless it is announced by a dream."

"And you expect me to believe that primitive nonsense?"

"Do you believe in radio and television? If electromagnetic waves can travel through space at a speed of three hundred thousand kilometers per second, why shouldn't the soul be able to do that?"

"God as transmitter and the soul as antenna," I said mockingly.

"Something like that. But not all souls are tuned to the right frequency. In that case the reception is faulty and the message is misunderstood."

Irritated, I shrugged my shoulders.

"The Torah abounds with dreams," Mr. Apfelschnitt continued. "How did Joseph arouse the anger of his brothers and how did he get into Egyptian captivity? Through dreams! To what did he owe his liberation? To dreams! Our forefathers dreamt a lot. And they took their dreams seriously, the good ones as well as the bad ones. Not long ago, it was the custom to fast for a whole day after a nightmare. If I'm not mistaken, there is even a special prayer that should be said after a bad dream."

He walked to his bookcase to look it up, but I stopped him, thanking him for the effort, which would be wasted on me.

r. Kalman continued to ignore my existence. He tolerated my presence only
because his wife employed me and because
he knew that nannies don't grow on trees. My indepen-
dence caused turmoil in his Orthodox family. Everything that I did or said was questionable from the very
start. The blessing of the Almighty couldn't possibly rest
on me since I did not ask for His blessing. I was as
unclean as a leper, or even worse; a leper is the innocent
victim of an illness, while I willfully rejected heavenly
mercy.

My affection for Simcha bothered his father. Mr.
Kalman was irritated that I, who embodied all the sins

from which he wanted to protect his children, shared his feelings for his youngest son. Was I expected to love Simcha? I was paid only to change diapers and to push the baby carriage through the park. No more was asked of me.

It was different for Mrs. Kalman. Listening to the unconventional stories that I told Simcha, she often had to smile. And when I raced through the apartment, neighing loudly with Simcha on my back while she was kneading bread dough at the kitchen table, I would catch a twinkle in her black eyes. Did our games amuse her? Did she feel pleased by the fact that I preferred Simcha to her other children, who were so much more beautiful and lovable? Perhaps she was relieved to hear Simcha, with his serious, little-old-man's head, laughing out loud. Perhaps my attachment to the child strengthened her own feelings for him. At any rate she granted me, silently and at a distance, but no less generously, the freedom to love him in my own way, although she could not approve of it openly. In this way a certain understanding slowly developed between us.

"Chaya," she asked one day, "would you be able to come and take care of the children this Thursday evening? My husband and I have to go somewhere together—we'll be back at eleven o'clock. After your work you can eat with us. That way you won't have to go home in between."

Although I didn't look forward to having a meal in the company of her forbidding husband, the prospect of being with Simcha longer than usual enticed me. On Thursday evening, after Tzivya and Esha had been put to bed, we all sat down to dinner. My heart pounded in my throat. Under the chilling glances of Mr. Kalman, I was conscious of every move I made.

We ate onion soup. Through the open kitchen window, the summertime sounds from the gardens below reached us. In the kitchen there sounded only the hollow click of our spoons. Avrom giggled.

"What did you learn in school today?" asked his father.

"We read Psalm one hundred twenty-one," he answered. " 'Behold, He that keepeth Israel doth neither slumber nor sleep.' "

"Good," Mr. Kalman nodded, satisfied.

"Yes," said Avrom, "but if it is true that the Eternal never sleeps, why is it written that He rested on the seventh day?"

"The Hebrew verb 'to rest' also means 'to cease' or 'to stop' doing something. Therefore, on the seventh day He ceased his work of creation."

"And what did He do after He had ceased his work?" asked Avrom as his mother put a big platter of herring salad on the table and began to cut bread to serve with it.

"As far as the Torah mentions and as far as I know, He did nothing."

"Doesn't that mean that He rested?"

"Probably, but it is possible to rest without sleeping," explained Mr. Kalman. "I'm resting now. And yet I'm wide-awake."

"You're not resting," said Avrom, "you're eating."

"True," his father said impatiently, "and I suggest that you do the same."

The salad of chopped herring, potatoes, and red beets tasted just like my mother's. I winked at Simcha, who sat diagonally across from me. Mr. Kalman and I reached for bread at the same time. I quickly pulled back my hand.

"And you, Dov? What did you do today?"

"We listened to a story. Mr. Saidel told us how Rabbi Judah Loew made the golem and how it protected the Jews of Prague against the *goyim*. I'd like to make a golem myself. You just need sand and water."

"You must have dreamed that," said his father. "At any rate, it won't work with sand and water. You'll just get mud on your clothes, and your mother already has plenty of laundry."

"What if I do it very carefully, without making a mess?"

Mr. Kalman laughed, "No human being can create a golem. Perhaps it once was possible, but that knowledge has been lost." Calmly he took a few bites of herring salad and then continued. "According to legend, the golem of Rabbi Loew was made of the purest mountain clay, which contained not even one pebble or a piece of straw. From this clay, in the running water of the Moldau, he kneaded the shape of a person. He baked it in a fire until the clay was hard. Then he buried the golem in the earth."

"Why?" Dov wanted to know.

"Why, why?" Mr. Kalman had laid down his fork and knife and held up his hands like someone who wants to check whether it's raining. "You shouldn't ask me that, I've never made a golem! According to the legend, it happened like that."

"And then?"

"Then he walked in a circle, not once but hundreds of times, around the spot where the golem was buried, while uttering the same words over and over."

"Which words?"

"That doesn't matter. It is forbidden to take part in such things. It's sorcery."

"But didn't Rabbi Chanina also do it?" said Avrom, his cheeks flushed with excitement. "Together with another rabbi he conjured a calf secretly at night. Just like that, from nothing. It was three times smaller than a normal calf. I read it myself."

"Didn't I tell you to eat?" his father said sharply. "So eat, my child, eat. And for pity's sake, don't forget to chew thoroughly with your mouth closed."

He then turned back to Dov. "The story of the golem who protects the Jews against injustice is lovely. But it's only a story. Only the Eternal One, blessed be His Great Name, can protect us."

"I know that," said Dov, "but I don't want a golem to protect us at all. I want him as a robot, to do my math and to learn Torah."

Mr. Kalman wiped his mouth. "Maybe a golem can do arithmetic. But learn Torah? For that you need a soul. And a golem has no soul, unless it is a soul of clay."

For him this ended the conversation. He was lost in thought until the end of the meal when we said the prayers. With bright voices, the children started the Hebrew hymn of thanksgiving with a cheerful staccato:

*When God returned us to Zion from exile*
*we were as in a dream.*
*Then our mouth filled with laughter*
*and cheers were on our tongue.*

But toward the end, the melody became compelling and melancholy. While we were singing, the same song sounded, like an echo, from one of the gardens under the window:

*Blessed is the man who trusts the Lord.*
*Once I was young and now I am old,*
*yet in all my days I never saw a righteous man abandoned*
*and his children begging for bread.*

After their parents had left, the boys ran around wildly. Avrom wanted never to sleep again, like the Eternal. And Dov, who imitated his brother in everything, was also bent on staying awake.

"Very well," I said. "You may stay awake, as long as you do so in bed."

They dragged together all the pillows from the whole apartment.

"We'll put them behind our backs so that we can sit up straight," explained Avrom.

Later, when I was sitting on the couch in the living

room, Simcha appeared. His red hair stuck to his fore-head and his cheeks were tear-stained.

"I want to keep my eyes open," he complained, "but they keep closing. Avrom says that I can't play with them and that the golem is coming to get me. And he took away my pillow."

I put aside my book and lay down on my side.

"Come," I said, pulling him toward me. "We're just ordinary people; we don't have to stay awake."

He nestled against me.

With short gasps, as though he were sobbing, he fell asleep in my arms. Our situation had something piti-ful about it, for which I was ashamed. It was as if I were looking down at us from a great height, the way we were lying there, on that ugly couch, in that bare room, under that harsh light. How had I come to be here? What was this strange child doing in my arms? I bent over him. His nostrils trembled, but the rest of his face was still. I studied the smooth eyelids with their delicate orange fringes.

Simcha Kalman. A three-year-old toddler with sidecurls and a beard. The beard didn't show yet, but it seemed as though it might break through the child's ten-der skin at any moment. Simcha had been born with a beard, just like his father, his grandfather, and his fore-bears of generations immemorial.

Simcha Kalman. I would have loved to let him discover my world, a world that was much larger than the cramped apartment, the park, and the bit of street between them. Before his eyes had stared themselves half blind on the Torah, the Talmud, and the prayer books, I wanted to teach him to wave to the boats on the Scheldt. I wanted to take him along to eat warm waffles on Meir Square, to see the marionettes in the Poesjenellenkelder, and in the evening to listen to the music of the carillon player in the clock tower on Groenplaats. But I knew that I was wishing for the impossible. He was locked into an existence with a radius for action not larger than the two thousand biblical ells of which Avrom had spoken. I had to love him as he was, within those limits.

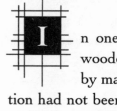 n one of my parents' rooms stood a large wooden loom that my mother had ordered by mail from Sweden years ago. Its installation had not been easy. A box of parts had arrived but without assembly instructions. For evenings on end my father tried in vain to put the thing together.

"Can you think of anything else?" he reproachfully demanded of my mother.

"You aren't handy at all," she answered, examining the results of his efforts with disdain. "It looks like a medieval instrument of torture."

"Perhaps that's what it is! Are you sure you ordered a loom?"

After a week he gave up.

"Do you know the story of the worker in Hitler's Germany?" he asked me. "He worked in a factory where parts for baby carriages were made. When his wife became pregnant, he decided to smuggle parts home, little by little, since he didn't earn enough to buy a baby carriage. Finally he had collected all the parts, and he went to the attic to put them together. Hours later, he comes downstairs, disheartened. 'I just don't understand it,' he says to his wife, 'no matter what I do, it always comes out a machine gun.'" My father pointed at the unsuccessful loom and sighed. "Now I understand how that man felt."

Soon after, having been delayed at customs, a second box from Sweden was delivered. It contained the missing parts as well as the instructions.

With the loom finally in her possession, my mother spent about three hours of every day weaving. She developed a preference for Bedouin motifs in which black and red predominated. All the chairs were upholstered in this fabric. The apartment became filled with bright colored carpets, wall hangings, and bedspreads. Still, she continued weaving. She liked to have people watch her, but we showed little interest in her work. Once in a while, when I had to ask her something urgently, I entered the weaving room. In the beginning,

I was surprised at the ugliness of the fabric, with its stubbly threads of beginning and ending. It was only after she cut the completed carpet from its thin scaffolding that the pattern appeared. Then, in the living room, glowing with satisfaction, she knotted the warp threads, two by two, into fringes.

"Do you see those colors?" she would exclaim. "What colors!"

One Sunday morning in June, when I visited my parents' apartment, I found only my mother at home. As soon as I sat down on the sofa, she placed a book in my lap, *The History of Navajo Weaving*. It consisted mainly of illustrations of traditional Navajo cloth.

"Note that characteristic sawtooth shape," she said, moving her index finger respectfully along the serrated lines, "and the diamond motif." She was standing behind me and quickly leafed from one illustration to the next. I blocked her hand in order to take a better look at a nineteenth-century photo of a loom. The loom consisted of warp threads strung beween two tree trunks, and the beginning of a carpet was visible upon it. A kneeling Navajo woman held the weaver's comb. All around her sheep were grazing.

"In 1864 Kit Carson solved the Navajo problem once and for all," I read aloud. "Under his leadership and by using scorched-earth tactics, the supply sheds, the cattle, and the orchards of the Navajo people were destroyed. The eight thousand Indians who surrendered went as prisoners of war on foot to Fort Sumner in the eastern part of New Mexico, where they were given numbered identity tags. Finally they ended in Bosque Redondo, a barren and desolate reservation that was hundreds of kilometers away from their place of birth."

My mother turned the page quickly. "The Navajo used to make blankets that were woven so tightly," she said nervously, "that they were completely waterproof. I'm going to try that, too."

"Why?" I asked. "It doesn't rain inside, does it?"

She walked to the kitchen. "You never know," she said over her shoulder.

What did you never know? We drank coffee. My mother sighed.

"It's good that you're here. Your father is out again, and the Goldblums are coming soon."

I told her that I had to work.

"Since when do you work at the flower shop on Sunday?"

"Not there, but at the Kalmans'."

"Do you go dressed like that, in old jeans and a faded blouse? They must really like that! And the dress I bought for you a while ago, do you ever wear it?"

I shook my head.

"You used to look so nice. Now you look like a wild woman. Do you think that men fall for that?"

"I don't care about men," I said. "But they certainly don't run away screaming when they see me. Not too long ago, two Chinese sailors were after me. And last week a Polish tourist asked me for directions, then said he wanted to take me to the movies, to the opera, and to get married."

"All in one day?"

"To escape him, I had to take a taxi. While it drove away, he sang to me."

"He sang to you? A Pole?" She shuddered.

"Yes, he danced and sang in the middle of the street. He really was a very nice man."

"And these elements are attracted to you? How primitive! Chinese sailors. Singing Poles. That never happened to me in my time."

"No, in your time the streets were infested with singing Germans."

She put down her cup and opened the book about the art of Navajo weaving again.

"You can never be normal and pleasant," she said, without looking at me. "You must get that from your father. He goes hunting for suitcases when he feels like it. And when he's home, he hardly opens his mouth."

"No wonder. Those suitcases keep him terribly busy. But as soon as he discusses it with you, you destroy all his illusions."

"Do I have to play along with this game? You know as well as I do that he'll never find those suitcases. I worry about him; I want to spare him the disappointment."

"You're the only one you worry about. Everything has to stay the same. Normal, pleasant. Being normal and nice is compulsory in this house. If anything threatens to be unpleasant, you go and bake a cake or weave watertight blankets."

"What do you have against pleasantness? Why can things be pleasant in other families but not in ours?"

"That's what you think. There are no pleasant families at all."

Fortunately, my father came home at that moment. He kissed my mother and then me. I didn't dare to ask about the suitcases, since he didn't look as though he'd made any progress.

"How are things?" I said.

He sighed. *"Ich bin ein Berliner."*

That sentence, once spoken by John F. Kennedy during his famous visit to Berlin, had begun to lead a life of its own in our house. At the time, when Kennedy's sentence made the papers, my father had burst out laughing. To the indignation of my mother who didn't understand what was so funny. "It should be *Ich bin Berliner,*" my father explained, laughing. "*Ich bin ein Berliner* means 'I am a jelly doughnut!'" At the thought of President Kennedy as a doughnut stuffed with jelly and sprinkled with powdered sugar, my mother and I also burst out laughing. The saying remained, first as a joke, but gradually it came to mean *Don't pay any attention to me, I've had it.* Or *Leave me alone.*

My father slumped into an easy chair. He must have walked for a long time. He was sweating and had even unbuttoned the top button of his shirt, a habit that he detested and found "low class" in others. I felt sorry for him and suddenly shared my mother's hope that he would stop his search.

"The Goldblums are coming in an hour," she said.

He rubbed his face. "That's all I need!" he said from the bottom of his heart. He especially disliked the heavily perfumed Mrs. Goldblum, who often complained about her marriage being childless and then would add in her broken Dutch, "My man, my man, he doesn't know that trick."

While my father went to wash up, I said goodbye to my mother and set out for the Kalmans' house.

**I**n the heat of the afternoon, Avrom and Dov chased after each other in the street. Simcha was leaning against the wall. His shirt hung out of his pants. He was playing with the white fringe of his *arba kanfot* and was lost in thought. It wasn't until my shadow fell across his face that he looked up. I bent down and kissed his forehead.

"*Noch amol.*" He smiled. Just as I leaned down again the concierge pounced on us. Without saying a word, he grabbed Simcha's arm and pulled the child indoors with him. Frightened, I ran after them. But when I entered the dark of the apartment house from the bright light outside, sunspots danced before my eyes. Blindly, I walked to the end of the hall where I could make out the silhouette of the man.

"Now I'll teach you once and for all how the elevator should be closed!" the concierge yelled angrily. He opened the cast-iron hinged gate, pressed Simcha's hand against the doorpost of the elevator, and was about to push the gate closed with full force on the hand.

Quick as lightning I put my foot in front of the gate, but he punched me with his elbow and made me stagger. In my fall, I grasped the collar of his work coat and hung on with my full weight. First the collar and then the whole back tore right through the middle, with a sharp sound as though a knife were cutting it. The concierge screamed, let go of Simcha's wrist, and kicked back like a donkey.

"Run up the stairs!" I shouted to Simcha, but he didn't seem to hear me. Dumbfounded, he stood still, watching our struggle. I dived suddenly under the arm of the concierge, grabbed Simcha around the waist, and got him and myself to the safety of the stairs.

"My coat is torn!" the concierge bellowed after us. "A coat of fifteen hundred francs!"

On the top step I turned around. My temples were pounding.

"Who do they think they are?" he roared at Attila, who sat yawning at a distance. "Every day I have to climb these damn stairs to get the elevator. I don't have to let myself be tormented by a bunch of Jews. I'm not getting paid for that!" He banged the gate of the elevator open and closed several times. "That's not my job," he shouted, "dammit, that's not my job!"

"Do you have other ambitions?" I said shrilly. "Are you thinking of perfecting the art of crushing children's hands?" From the bottom of the stairs he let out a stream of vulgar curses. I lifted Simcha in my arm. He weighed nothing. As though driven by steam, I carried him up the next five flights.

"Don't get excited," said Mrs. Kalman after I finished my story. "We don't want to quarrel with anyone, and least of all with the concierge. We can't go in or out of this house without passing by him."

"But he was ready to smash Simcha's hand!"

She squatted down and closely scrutinized Simcha's hands. There wasn't a scratch to be seen. "Come," she said, sighing, "I'll pour some tea."

"That man is dangerous," I insisted. "He calls us damned Jews. And now that I've torn his coat, he really hates us like the plague."

She shrugged her shoulders. "That's how it is. It's never been any different."

"If you resign yourself so easily, then it will never change!" I said sharply.

With trembling lips, I drank the tea. My teeth chattered against the edge of the glass.

"Is his coat really torn?" she asked me.

I nodded. "Yes, but I wouldn't dream of compensating him for the damage, if that's what you mean. I'd rather die!"

She laughed. "It is written that we should not rejoice in the fall of our enemy. But nowhere does it say that we have to help him back on his feet."

The fight with the concierge had affected Simcha more deeply than I realized. For the first time in weeks he wet his pants. When I was changing him, Avrom came into the bathroom and shouted excitedly that his brother absolutely needed to learn the blessing that Jewish men say while they are dressing.

"When you're putting on your pants you have to say, Blessed art Thou, Ruler of the World, who has not created me as woman."

Simcha burst into tears.

When Avrom started the blessing for the belt, his mother came in to chase him away. But from afar he shouted, "Blessed art thou, Ruler of the World, who girds Israel with strength."

When I entered my room toward six o'clock, the heat had almost reached the boiling point. To prevent the furniture from liquefying, I threw open all the windows. Then I undressed and pushed my head under the kitchen faucet. Lukewarm water, smelling of rust, streamed through my hair and ran in trickles over my back. It brought no cooling. Not a breath of air came through the windows. The heat remained standing in the room like a column.

My head was pounding. I was agitated about the concierge. And I was agitated about the fact that I was agitated about someone who was not worth my agitation, with the result that I became increasingly furious. Nauseated with fury, I stretched out on my bed. I rolled on my side and pulled up my knees. After a bit, my breathing became calmer, and my eyes closed. The last thing I saw was the book that I had been reading the night before. It lay on the table like a waiting lover.

I fell asleep and dreamed of a large synagogue. The blue mosaic walls were illuminated by candles. Hundreds of Hasidim in black caftans and fur hats stood in many long rows. I thought that they were praying. But when I looked more closely, I discovered that they were assaulting their prayer books. With lascivious gestures they turned page after page. Shamelessly, they stroked the paper or brought it to their lips. While uttering Hebrew sounds, they moved back and forth, ever wilder, until their books groaned and cooed with pleasure. A long drawn-out sigh went through the building, making the candle flames quiver.

The pigeons in the rain gutter awoke me. It was twilight. I dressed and walked to the Scheldt. Even there, there was no wind, but the nearness of the river gave the illusion of a certain coolness. With an iron mooring post as backrest, I sat at the water's edge. I thought back to the words that Avrom had shouted. *Blessed art Thou, Ruler of the World, who girds Israel with strength.* What was Israel's strength? For the Kalman family, it was not the strength to ward off danger, but to endure it. And what was meant by Israel? The Kalmans, in their almost hostile isolation? My father, with his argument for assimilation? My mother, for whom Judaism equaled pain? Mr. Apfelschnitt, who felt saved by it? Or all of them together?

According to the Torah, the Jews were charged by God to be a light unto the nations. But the Torah is behind the times. Nowadays even the Papuans and the Laplanders have light bulbs. To be chosen or exterminated. Between these two words stretch the centuries-old inability of the Jews to understand the world and the world's inability to understand the Jews. These were fatal words whose meaning I had never experienced myself. But I was familiar with the consequences that they had for the people around me. Being chosen or exterminated were confirming opposites in a conflict of Jewish identity of which I wanted no part.

And God? I had read somewhere that when an Eskimo traveled across the polar plain by himself, he would build at set distances an *inokok,* a heap of stones that from a distance looked like a human form. As he continued his journey, he would turn around several times to look at this stone shape. Perhaps he would wave to that thing, perhaps he'd talk to it under his breath, perhaps he'd sing songs to it at the top of his voice. And perhaps in time he was even able to see this alter ego wave back at him. In any case, that faraway, dark shape was there to prevent the emptiness of the snow-covered landscape from driving him mad with loneliness.

For Mr. Apfelschnitt, the Kalmans, and millions of others, God replaced the *inokok* of the Eskimo. They looked to Him, they spoke to Him, and they sang to Him. This they had done with such conviction and for so long that they had forgotten that they had created and animated Him, just as Rabbi Loew had brought the golem into being.

I was convinced that the concierge would take revenge. According to his primitive notions of cause and effect, I had not only his torn coat on my conscience but also, incidentally and very conveniently, his entire torn life as well.

On the evening after the incident, I had been able to leave the Kalmans' house without being noticed, but that kind of luck wouldn't strike twice. I expected him to lash out at me the following day as I entered the house.

He didn't disappoint me. I had barely reached the stairs when he rushed at me.

"That torn coat has to be paid for," he hissed.

"That's going to cost you fifteen hundred francs."

"It doesn't seem to be all that urgent," I said calmly. "I see that you're wearing another one."

"Of course I'm wearing another one! I have two coats, and every week one is in the laundry. How else could it be, with all the filth here!"

"I'm not planning to give you fifteen hundred francs."

He gnashed his teeth in fury. "Then I'll lodge a complaint with the owner in Brussels."

"You must do what you can't help," I said while stepping on the lowest tread of the stairs. "And do tell him also that the coat in question was torn while you were busy beating up one of the residents of this house."

I walked upstairs, deaf to his impotent ranting.

He addressed me a few more times. On my departure for the park with the children, he danced around me like a boxer. "If I understand you correctly, you're not planning to reimburse me for the coat?" he asked, threatening. I nodded in agreement and he disappeared from view.

Upon our return he took another tack. As I walked to the elevator with Esha, he said obsequiously, "You must think that my coats are paid for by the landlord. In that case, you're completely wrong. I have to pay for everything out of my salary, including soap flakes and polishing wax. Every nail that I hammer into a wall I pay for out of my salary."

"And every crack in the ceiling is filled with your own blood," I said. "Yes, life isn't easy."

"You make fun of it, but I need a coat to do my job. How else would people recognize me? At the very least I need a coat! Do you know that caretakers used to wear a uniform?"

"With or without decorations?" I asked, impatiently rocking the baby in my arms.

For an instant he was confused. Then, offended, he stalked away so fast that Attila couldn't keep up.

With that, the matter ended. Or so I thought. I was feeding Tzivya and Esha some mashed fruit, and the concierge too seemed to have resumed his routine. When I went down the stairs to get the baby carriage, I found him lugging a big table. It was a relief to hear him grumbling as before. "Move over, Attila, move over! Get out of my way, it's very heavy. I can feel all the blood flowing to my feet again. 'Don't work too hard,' the doctor says. What does the doctor know about work? He doesn't have to lift tables, he has a staff."

By the time I stepped out of the elevator after work, the hall was so full of furniture that I could hardly pass.

An old-fashioned wardrobe had been pushed at a right angle against the wall, leaving me just enough room to get by. However, just as I tried to wriggle sideways through the opening, I found it blocked by something else. Wasn't that the table the concierge had been struggling with an hour before? Placed on its narrow side with the top facing me, it blocked the opening to eye level. The concierge, half a head taller than I, could just look over it.

"If you will now please give me fifteen hundred francs," he said triumphantly, "I might be kind enough to let you go through!"

I looked from the cupboard to the table. I had immediately thought that the furniture looked like a barricade, but it took a while for me to realize that it was actually meant as such. What should I do? Throw myself against it? Climb over it? I didn't want to grant Mr. Caretaker that satisfaction. Was there no other way out? I tiptoed through the hall and quietly I tried the door handles, one after the other, but they were all locked.

I thought of the story of the Baal Shem Tov, about the palace with the imaginary walls. Was it possible to break down walls by sheer mental power? Perhaps in the lofty regions of the spirit. But in the material world, where idiots wield the scepter, the walls are all too real, just like the idiots themselves, for that matter. After I had listened for a while to the snickering of the concierge, who was gloating on the other side of the cupboard, I turned around and stepped back into the elevator.

Mrs. Kalman didn't seem surprised or angry at all. She was afraid of the anger of the concierge and again suggested reimbursing him for the torn coat. She got fifteen hundred francs from the buffet, but I refused to accept the money.

"Then I'll go and give it to him myself," she said.

"If you do that, I'll never come to work here again."

She sighed. "If only my husband were here, he could go and talk with him. But he's in Switzerland on business."

"There's no point in talking. The concierge speaks another language."

"True, he doesn't speak Yiddish, but my husband does speak Flemish."

"No, that's not what I mean. With the concierge, dialogue is impossible in any language. He is another being."

"He is a *goy*."

"Not all *goyim* are like the concierge, Mrs. Kalman! I know that in this city there are quite a few *goyim* who don't care for Jews, but that doesn't mean that they attack Jewish children or construct barricades. The concierge has a screw loose."

"That may be true," she answered, "but it may also be your fault. We've lived here for five years, and we've never had a problem with him."

"He calls you a Jewish pig, he mistreats your children, and he baits your employee, but you've never had a problem with him?"

"In all these years, nothing serious has ever happened, nothing that is serious enough to lose sleep over."

"What do you consider sufficiently serious? Manslaughter? Premeditated murder?"

"I don't want to hear any more about it," she said. "You can sleep here tonight and tomorrow we'll see again. We mustn't force the issue."

"The issue has been forced—by the concierge. I won't even consider sleeping here. It solves nothing. Tomorrow that furniture will still be in the hall. And then? Will I have to beg on my knees to go past it? I want to go home now and not when it suits the concierge. I'm not letting myself be locked in!"

Trembling with anger, I first walked to the boys' bedroom and then to the kitchen since both rooms were located at the back of the house. Mrs. Kalman lost some of her icy calm.

"You're not going outside through the window, are you? That's much too dangerous. Besides, there's chicken wire in front of it."

"I can loosen chicken wire easily enough."

"And the children? Do you want to set a bad example for the children?"

"It may just be a very good example."

"To fall down from the fourth floor and break your neck?"

"No, to show them that I won't let myself be pushed around by the concierge."

"You let him do that much more than we do. We don't let ourselves be provoked, but you tear his coat and cause difficulties, not only for yourself but also for us."

She chased Avrom and Dov, who were listening eagerly, to the living room and said, "Every day I warn the boys to stay away from the windows. If you climb out through them, they'll never take my warning seriously again!"

"Then you can tell them that it's not dangerous for me because I'm a witch. I already have such a bad name in this family. What do you call me again? Gomer?"

Tears sprang to her eyes. "That's not fair. You've never heard me say such a thing. Perhaps my husband, yes, but he means well. It makes him unhappy that you are so self-willed and that you do things that are forbidden for Jewish women."

"The Holy Scripture teems with self-willed women," I said. "Without the help of Rebecca, Jacob would never have been able to steal the right of the first-born from his brother. Deborah administered justice between Rama and Bethel. And I, Mrs. Kalman, am going out through your kitchen window, whether you like it or not."

She mumbled something about the support of the Almighty and left the kitchen, wringing her hands. I pulled loose a corner of the chicken wire that covered most of the window. A downspout ran beside the window. If I lowered myself one floor, I would be able to step on the flat roof of a neighbor. I looked over my shoulder.

There is an almost rustic anarchy to the courtyards of Antwerp. Houses with identical facades have nothing in common in the back. One sees an untidy collection of balconies, projecting entresols, angled and rounded bay windows, glass domes, and assorted additions stubbornly competing with one another. In a maze of fences below there is everything from a pathetic tiled court to a lush vegetable garden complete with chickens.

When I had one leg around the downspout and still had the other foot on the window sill, Simcha appeared.

The well-worn fringe of his *arba kanfot* stuck out from under his shirt.

"Are you leaving?" he asked softly.

"Yes, I can't stay."

"Because you have to go to the ducks?"

"No, because I don't have a toothbrush with me."

"Are you climbing up to the roof?"

I shook my head and pointed down.

He quacked and with his index finger he stroked my foot on the window sill.

*"Ave Caesar,"* I said, looking into the depth, *"moritori te salutant."*

"What are you saying?"

"It's a magic spell, not to fall. Now quickly move away from the window."

He remained standing. While I let myself slip down, his pale face with the bright red hair disappeared slowly behind the window ledge, like a sun sinking behind the horizon. Meanwhile I scraped myself on the jagged clips attaching the downspout to the wall. With bleeding feet I jumped on to the flat roof. I wasn't very good at climbing, but the necessity of my flight and the victory over the concierge inspired me to great efforts. Without the least hesitation, I clambered over high fences and rickety sheds. When I reached the street, dirty and with a tear in my jeans, I was sorry that my escapade was over.

The next afternoon, Mrs. Kalman was waiting for me at the corner of Simons Street. She was holding Simcha's hand and looking nervous. It seemed better to her that I not come to work for a week. Upon my return, she said, the concierge would have cooled off. I protested, but her decision was firm. She herself would take care of Simcha and the twins. I would continue to be paid, so I shouldn't be dissatisfied. But I was. What she smilingly called a truce had for me the bitter taste of capitulation.

The afternoons without Simcha dragged on. I stolled along the Scheldt and hung around listlessly in the Museum of Fine Arts. I spent hours in a room with paintings by James Ensor. Sitting on a bench, I stared at the *Entry of Christ into Brussels*, a large canvas on which Christ himself is barely visible, since he is surrounded by a frenzied mob. Among the rabble I recognized the face of the detested concierge more than once. The populace seemed to consist entirely of such unsavory types.

n one of those dreary days, I went to pour out my heart to Mr. Apfelschnitt. I arrived just as he was about to say his morning prayer. From the sofa near the window I watched him while he took out his prayer straps. He rolled up the left sleeve of his shirt and placed one of the prayer boxes on his upper arm so that it pointed toward the heart. Then he said the blessing and started to wrap the long black strap around his arm. Silently I watched as he tied the second box on his forehead and blessed it as well. Then he rocked his upper body forward and back, forward and back, as he began the Shema: "Hear, O Israel, the Lord our God, the Lord is One." In *Scientific American* I had read that from the back and forth motion of a praying Jew a cardiologist could tell the rhythm of his heartbeat. But I became so sleepy from watching Mr. Apfelschnitt's movements that my eyes almost closed.

It wasn't until later, when he sat down facing me, that I shook off that lethargy. I told him about the concierge, his floods of abuse, his tampering with the baby carriage, and his attack on Simcha. Gradually, I became angry all over again. I told him that I found Mrs. Kalman's reaction incomprehensible.

"She lets that man get away with murder. I've never seen her or her husband protest anything. Where is it written that they have to watch without complaining as their children are being mistreated?"

"Nowhere," answered Mr. Apfelschnitt. "The old rabbis were not proponents of violence, but they recognized that its use is sometimes unavoidable. They said that when someone is planning to attack, kill, or physically harm another person, a third party doesn't have only the right but also the duty to prevent this, with force if necessary. The concierge can thank his lucky stars that he escaped unscathed." He got up to pour himself a glass of vodka. "In the Talmud there most certainly is a discussion about the necessity of self-defense," he said. Then he tipped the glass, emptying it down his throat. "The fact that so many Jews let themselves be chased into the gas chambers by Eichmann is not a logical consequence of our religion but of our history. For two thousand years we have survived Christian violence, from Byzantine persecution through the massacres of the Crusaders, from the Spanish Inquisition through the Russian czars. We were able to take blow after blow and struggle to our feet again every time. Because of that, the idea took hold that we were invulnerable, not as individuals but as a people. The Jewish people, it was said, could not be destroyed." He poured another glass. "And how did we survive? Not by hitting back, but my making ourselves as small as possible. We, who revered David because he had slain the giant Goliath, threw ourselves at the feet of the grand duke to beg for his benevolence. We, who proudly told our children how Samson had killed a thousand Philistines, crawled in the dirt for the mayor and his most insignificant pencil-pushers. No tax was too high, no humiliation too low. We remained standing by bending. Was an army of Crusaders coming to massacre us? No problem! Jewish compliance went so far that we withdrew into our houses and personally set them afire. Pleading and compromising had become second nature to us. How could we know that there was no pleading with the likes of Himmler and Eichmann? Naturally, there was resistance, in the ghettos and even in the camps, but that came much too late, and it resulted in about a few hundred dead Germans."

He sighed and picked up his glass. "Do you know," he said, "that I used to be able to dance the hora with a glass of vodka on my head? Without spilling a drop! No use trying that now. I thank God that I can tie my shoelaces without losing my balance." He laughed, but I didn't join in.

"What's the matter?" he asked. "Is the concierge still bothering you?"

First I shrugged my shoulders, but then I agreed. "Sometimes I think it's my fault," I said glumly.

"What is your fault?"

"That everywhere I run into people who are prejudiced against Jews. Sometimes they're just ignorant, but they all happen to cross my path. I meet them among the students, on the street, or when I go to a café. As though I attract them like a magnet."

"Nonsense. You stumble across anti-Semites because they live in this city and because you move around in this city. They're as numerous as sparrows. How often do you see a sparrow?"

"Every day. Several."

"Do you conclude from this that you exert a mysterious attraction on sparrows?"

I shook my head.

"Nevertheless, there are also good people among them," said Mr. Apfelschnitt. "How could we live here otherwise? We have what you could call a real Jewish quarter."

"As though that weren't possible in Amsterdam or even in Berlin!"

"I don't know whether it's possible in those places, I'm not so sure of that at all. At any rate, it's possible in Antwerp. We may not be exactly loved here, but we are more or less tolerated, with all our idiosyncrasies."

"Are we so peculiar? Then the anti-Semites are right!"

He chuckled.

"Surely the Hasidim behave more peculiarly than any of us," I said seriously. "With those caftans and those beards, it's no wonder people point at them in the street."

"Maybe," said Mr. Apfelschnitt, "but they don't complain about it, do they? You yourself say that the Kalmans do nothing against that criminal of a concierge. They endure everything: ridicule, hate, revulsion. That's the price they pay to remain who they are."

"My father thinks the Hasidim are backward. According to him, they don't uphold Judaism so much as the existence of the ghetto. He maintains that

Judaism owes its continued survival to flexibility and adaptability."

"I think Judaism still exists and will continue to exist because it's the only religion that promises redemption in exchange for critical thinking. In Judaism, belief always quarrels with logic. That tension is not fought but encouraged. In other religions that is less usual, to say it politely. But flexibility and adaptability? These qualities certainly didn't contribute to the survival of the Jews. From the time of the Enlightenment, Jews have done their best to assimilate. We let ourselves be baptized and changed our names. We systematically denied and effaced our own nature, at least in confrontation with the outside world, since among ourselves most of us remained as Jewish as chicken soup with matzah balls. We have suffered from pathological indecision. Who or what are we really? In the mirror that is held up to us by the world, we have been scoundrels. In our own mirror we have been prophets and saints. We wanted to erase the image of scoundrel but couldn't let go of the presumption of holiness. And while we were jumping from one foot to the other, Hitler came along to decide our fate. He did the opposite. He blew our evil image into proportions compared to which Beelzebub resembled a toddler and chased the remainder of holiness to which we held fast through the chimneys. The essence of assimilation: we dissolved into air." He shook his head. "No," he said, "there is no other people who has made such great concessions to be allowed, please, to belong to humanity. We haven't succeeded."

"But how can there ever be equality among people if we don't conform?"

"Equality, equality!" he shouted impatiently. "That sounds very nice, but God forbid that we all become equal. Do you want to be equal to the concierge who attacked you?" He peered into his vodka. "It wasn't for nothing that Noah was commanded to load examples of all living creatures into his ark, from every kind of bird to every kind of cattle. For each kind has its own purpose on Earth. If one is missing, Creation is no longer complete. That's how it is with people. We each have our own destiny, but we are all together in the ark. There is no trick to loving your neighbor if he resembles you in every way. What counts is to reach out to one another, even though we are completely different. Only then can we turn the tide."

"Will we ever succeed?" I asked.

He squeezed his eyes into slits.

"Never," he answered grimly.

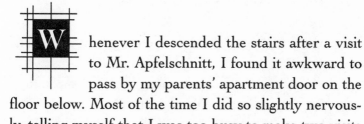 henever I descended the stairs after a visit to Mr. Apfelschnitt, I found it awkward to pass by my parents' apartment door on the floor below. Most of the time I did so slightly nervously, telling myself that I was too busy to make two visits on one day. But today I stopped and rang the bell. My mother opened the door.

"Why don't you just use your key to let yourself in?" she said.

"I don't want to surprise you at an inconvenient time."

She laughed, mocking. "In that case you should leave right away, since all moments are equally inconvenient here ever since your father began trying to find those suitcases."

"What do you mean?" I asked, following her to the living room.

Once there, she turned angrily. "What do I mean? As if you care! You live only for yourself! Every six or seven weeks you come by. And why? To see whether we're still living here? You can save yourself the trouble. If we move, you'll receive a change of address notice!"

"Do you ever visit me?"

"You've never invited us."

"Not true."

"Yes, but then you mentioned in the same breath that you have mice."

"They live in the house next door. At most they come once in a while to take a peek."

"I don't like mice, not even mice who just take a peek."

With tears in her eyes she distractedly plumped up one of her handwoven pillows, picked a piece of fluff from the floor, and moved an ashtray on the table. When she began to pick withered leaves from a hanging plant, I said, "What's happening with the suitcases?"

I flopped down on the sofa. She remained standing, one hand holding the dead leaves.

"He says the digging has started, I don't know where. I don't even know whether he's having it done or whether he's digging himself. I know absolutely nothing, and I don't ask about it either."

"Then why are you so worried? Whether he finds them or not, he can't keep digging forever. Before you know it, he'll be playing chess again in Café Berkowitz."

"No," she said reflecting. "No. He's changed so much, he's become so determined. He insists that he must have those suitcases. And the more he struggles, the smaller the chance becomes that he'll ever dig them up."

"It doesn't seem entirely impossible."

"That's because you're just like him. When you get an idea, you lose all sense of proportion." She gestured in the direction of the table, as though he were sitting there. "All that looking at city maps, all that reckoning! And in the end he goes off with a piece of paper that looks like a primitive treasure map from a boys' book!" Through the balcony doors she looked at the street below. "Even if he finds them, things will never be all right again. He didn't start all this because of his violin or the old photos. He thinks that these suitcases will be able to give back to him what the war destroyed: Berlin, his youth, his father and mother, everything that he had and was. It's not his suitcases but he himself who got lost in that damned war. And all of us as well. We're all missing." She was crying. "Oh, God, he's digging for himself in this eighty-five-degree heat!"

She stood sobbing, with her back to me. For the first time she had said something to me about the war. But she hadn't talked about it, she had let it slip. I looked at her shaking shoulders. She seemed more distant than a Vietnamese woman I had once seen on a television news report, who cried out so loud to heaven over the dead child in her arms that I wondered why the sun, the moon, and all the stars did not flee from her lamentation. That nameless woman, at the other end of the world, had been closer to me than my mother would ever be.

Suddenly, she was fiddling with the pleats of a curtain. Then, avoiding me, she walked to the kitchen. A few minutes later, she returned cheerfully, carrying tea and poppy-seed cookies.

We talked about anything and everything. Was I still working for the Hasidic family? Were my studies going well? Did I also think that Jacov Apfelschnitt had become very thin?

"Did I tell you yet that the Goldblums have separated?"

"At their age?"

She nodded. "You know that he collected postage stamps?"

Of course I knew that. He'd been doing it for twenty-five years, and as I saw it, he'd talked about nothing else for twenty-five years.

"They had a fight, I don't know about what," said my mother. "And when he came home in the evening, she was gone. But before leaving she had pasted his whole stamp collection on the walls. All his stamps, every single one!"

"In that living room of theirs, with that hideous wallpaper? That could only be an improvement."

"Can you imagine? She must have been busy doing it all day. Licking and pasting, licking and pasting."

"My man, my man, he doesn't know that trick!" we shouted simultaneously.

While we were laughing ourselves weak, my father appeared suddenly in the doorway. His shirt sleeves were rolled up. The shirt itself was full of sand and hung open in the front. On his red sunburned chest, which glistened with sweat, his scars stood out like white hieroglyphs. He pointed over his shoulder. "I've got company."

Behind him two policemen surfaced, smiling politely. "Good afternoon," said one. He took my father by the elbow and helped him into a chair.

"The gentleman didn't have his identity card with him," said the other apologetically to my mother.

"It's in the inside pocket of my jacket," my father said, without looking at her.

Upset, she left the room and brought back not only the identity card but the jacket as well, as if to prove that the card had indeed been in the pocket in question. The policemen hardly looked at it.

"This afternoon we were called because this gentleman, your husband, was digging a hole in soil that is private property," declared the older one of the two. He threw my mother a questioning glance. "The manager of the property had enjoined him to leave, but he refused. He said he was searching for two valises. Then we became involved and talked with him. "

He turned toward my father and placed a hand on his shoulder. "Valises from the war, isn't that right, sir?" he said in a loud voice as though he were speaking to a deaf person.

"That's correct," my mother answered quickly. "They were buried in nineteen forty-three, when there were still houses there. My husband was hidden there."

The policeman nodded. "The gentleman was perhaps in the Resistance?" He again patted my father's shoulder clumsily. "Or Jewish?"

"Both," answered my mother. "Later he was caught and put on transport."

"Yes, yes," the policeman said with compassion.

"But the city has changed a lot in twenty-seven years. If the valises were there, you would have found them. You've dug up enough soil. Without a permit."

His colleague felt equally uncomfortable. "We'll solve it," he assured us. "The damage isn't much. You'll receive the bill, and that will be the end of the matter. But if you start digging again tomorrow or next week, then you'll make things difficult for us. We'll have to take other measures, whether we like it or not. Do you understand?"

My father nodded.

"After all, Antwerp is not a sandbox. If everyone were to start digging here and there, nothing would be left. That's why we're going to take possession of your shovel."

They said goodbye to my father kindly, almost tenderly. My mother let them out. When she returned, she stroked my father's damp hair.

He stared ahead, glassy-eyed. "I don't know what I should do," he said.

"Take a bath, change clothes, drink a cup of coffee," she answered calmly.

"No, after that!" It sounded desperate. "I don't know what I should do after that!"

"After that? Eat, sleep, read a book, play chess."

"But I've already done that for years!"

"Indeed. And you'll continue doing it for years."

She tried to kiss him, but he evaded her. Then she lost patience.

"Now listen, if you had found these suitcases, wouldn't there also follow another day, and another, and another? Wouldn't you have to eat and sleep then as well?"

"Yes, but it would be different."

"Nonsense! Even a hundred suitcases would change nothing. We don't change any more, and our lives don't change any more. Tomorrow you'll play chess again and I'll go on with my weaving."

He heaved a sigh and quoted Heine: *"O Germany, at your shroud we sit. / We're weaving a threefold curse in it. / We're weaving, we're weaving."*

While my mother went to fill the bathtub, he sat facing me silently. He didn't know how to conceal his embarrassment.

"You think I'm a real fool, right?"

I shook my head.

"When I was younger, at school," I told him, "the children were always bragging about their fathers. My father went on a safari and captured a tiger! My father is a champion boxer! All lies! The only one with an interesting father was Jan Selie, because he had a candy store. And I, I had you. You had danced in a real movie, but I couldn't tell anyone, because they wouldn't believe me anyway. Their fathers would shit in their pants at the mere thought of all that you had done. Fleeing without a penny in your pocket. Starting again in a new country, among strangers, in a strange language. And later in an SS uniform, putting one over on the Germans, forging papers on a large scale, saving people while being in danger yourself. Those things—hiding, going into and out of concentration camps—it would have been much easier to catch a tiger."

Was he listening? His gaze was turned inward.

"I think you've really been a dancer all your life. You didn't actually do these things but danced them. And the suitcases were just a mistake. Can't a dancer make a mistake?"

"Not at my age," he said, rubbing his face with both hands. "I'm finished dancing."

My mother came in to get him for his bath. She sent me to the bakery to buy a sacher torte, because, she whispered as she slipped me five hundred francs, "That does him good."

I t was a long week. How often—while I was working in the restaurant or at the flower shop—had I not longed to take off for the city, just to stroll around from bookstore to bookstore, or to eat a freshly baked coffee cake while sitting on one of the benches in the quiet garden behind the Rubens house. Now that I finally had time, I wasted it, out of a certain stubbornness. Freedom is lovely, but it shouldn't be compulsory.

I also missed Simcha's company. Without him I felt like Robinson Crusoe, abandoned by Friday, once more alone on my island. The days crept by. I no longer felt like reading. In the end, I mostly lay on my bed, sometimes sleeping, and, when awake, cursing the persistent heat. When did Mrs. Kalman expect me back? She had said nothing about it, but I assumed that I would begin again on Sunday.

On Saturday evening I decided to fix myself up for the reunion with Simcha, and emptied my clothes closet for the occasion. What did I think I'd find? I wore most of the few clothes that I possessed with reluctance. Still, as though hoping that my clothes had mated in the darkness of the closet and had given life to something else besides worn jeans and T-shirts, I searched. My eye fell on a white silk jacket that my mother had discarded some time ago and that I'd never worn.

On Sunday morning I was too excited to eat. I was sitting at the table in my mother's jacket and with my hair braided, when the bell rang. Leaning out of a window I saw Mr. Apfelschnitt standing at the door. Quickly, I knotted the house key in a sock and threw it to him. While he climbed the eight flights of stairs, I made my bed and picked up a dirty washcloth and a shoe from the floor.

He appeared in the stairwell, panting. It wasn't until he had drunk a glass of water that he caught his breath. He sat uneasily on one of my hard wooden chairs. He looked at me helplessly, as though he suddenly realized that he had the wrong house as well as the wrong street and was now facing a total stranger.

"An uncle of mine taught me that you should never bring someone bad news without letting good news precede it. Whether that is a question of grace or cowardice, I leave up in the air. At any rate, I've made it a habit." He tugged nervously at one of his enormous gray eyebrows. "Therefore, first the good news," he said. "On Friday, your father played chess with me at Berkowitz's. We played four games. If you ask me, he's his old self again."

From the corner of my eyes I glanced at my old alarm clock. It was almost time to leave.

"And now the bad news." He took a deep breath and said, "Simcha Kalman is dead."

He said much more, but I didn't understand most of it. I did hear the squeaking of the tram stopping on the square, the voices of people in the street, the alarm clock ticking next to my head. But what Mr. Apfelschnitt told me penetrated only in fragments. Fire? Had he said something about fire? I thought of the recurring dream in which Simcha was slowly consumed by an unquenchable fire. And meanwhile the room filled with sounds. It was as if I were hearing even the distant wing beats of sea gulls above the Scheldt.

Mr. Apfelschnitt took hold of my arm. "How often

do I have to repeat it? Simcha has drowned! On Friday evening, his mother noticed that he had disappeared. Yesterday divers pulled him out of the pond in the park."

"How do you know that?"

"I know it because I was sitting on my bench, like every Saturday morning. When the men from the fire department came in their wetsuits, and when it became clear to me whom they were looking for, I stayed."

"Why didn't you come and get me?"

"You? To do what? There were plenty of people around, half the city had turned out. Almost all *goyim*, they have a good nose for misery. His father also stood there the whole morning, with a few other Belzer Hasidim. The rabbi was there, too. They canceled the Shabbat service."

"How can a child fall into the water without anyone seeing it? And how can you drown there? The pond isn't that deep at all, is it?"

He shrugged his shoulders. "Whoever is destined to drown will drown in a spoonful of water."

"But if no one saw it, how did the divers know to look for him in the pond?"

"Because on Friday evening his mother had found a toy of his at the water's edge. A wooden duck with wheels. His father stood holding it in his hands from the beginning until the end, as though he could get his child back with it."

While Mr. Apfelschnitt was answering my questions, Simcha was already buried or being buried. Jews bury their dead quickly. It is said that they do this out of respect for the deceased, whose body must never appear in decay. But I think that practical as they are, they've made a virtue of necessity. On occasion, a mourner might be able to sit beside a single body for days on end, sobbing or knitting, whereas the children of Israel, burdened throughout history with masses of dead at the same time, have learned to hurry and clean up the mess before the next pogrom. That's why they postpone the sitting until after the digging. But then the sitting is done with complete devotion. The mourners don't leave their house. Cared for by family members and friends, they sit close to the floor and as uncomfortably as possible for seven days.

I too remained sitting until long after Mr. Apfelschnitt's departure, not out of religious considerations, but because nothing else occurred to me. I sat, just staring at my hands on the table. It wasn't until the end of the afternoon that I realized that, as nanny, I should urgently go and offer my condolences to Simcha's parents. I couldn't postpone it until the next day because if I didn't do it now, I would never do it.

I went to the Kalmans that same evening and found them indeed sitting: Mr. Kalman on the floor, his wife and the boys on a low wooden bench. They were in the company of people unknown to me, some of whom were sitting on crates and others just on chairs. When I entered, they all stopped talking. Because it is the custom that visitors not speak until one of the mourners addresses them, I waited silently. The silence was suffocating. I was hoping for a look from Mrs. Kalman, a sign of recognition or greeting, but she kept her eyes lowered. I sat down on the edge of an easy chair, the same one in which Simcha had hidden from me at our first meeting. Dov and Avrom looked at me with hostility, while Mr. Kalman followed my movements with Argus eyes. He moaned several times.

When he finally spoke, he asked, "Why did you come here? Have you no respect at all, not even for the dead?"

I looked at him, shocked.

"It would be better if you left," whispered a thin Hasid near me. "No one wants to accuse you, certainly not on a day like today. But you're not really welcome here."

"Accuse me?" I said.

Mr. Kalman could no longer control himself. "Isn't it true that you let Simcha feed bread to the ducks every day? And that in doing this he almost fell into the water?" he shouted. "A child barely four years old who can't swim! Is that true or not?"

I nodded.

"After such an accident, people talk," he said bitterly. "Simcha never played with the other children in the park. You kept him apart, you sat with him on a bench and put who knows what evil ideas into his head. Half the day he walked around quacking, as though we had brought a duck into the world instead of a son! 'Don't mind it,' said my wife, 'it's just a game.' My wife is too kind, she always defended you. But I distrusted you from the moment that you came to work here!"

All eyes were on me. Only Mrs. Kalman still looked down.

"I should not speak like this," Mr. Kalman continued. "A person must resign himself to the will of the Almighty. Everything has its time and place, even evil. But that doesn't mean that I should admit evil into my house and watch it sit down in my best chair! No sane person can expect that of me!"

I wanted to say something, but he didn't give me a chance. As though there could be a doubt that I was the one to whom he was speaking, he pointed his finger at me. "Please leave! And be so kind as to use the staircase instead of the downspout!"

My face burning with shame, I stood up, preparing to walk the long distance to the door. But Mrs. Kalman rose as well. In two steps she was next to me. Silently she grasped the edge of my silk jacket at chest level, and there made the *keriah*, the ritual rending of a garment by mourners, reserved only for the immediate family of the dead. In her dark, red-rimmed eyes there shone a sweet triumph. Hoarsely, she recited a few lines from the praise of the righteous woman.

"Many daughters have done virtuously," she said, "but thou excellest them all." Then she laid her hands on my warm forehead and blessed me.

Downstairs I knocked in vain on the concierge's lodge. I found him in the boiler room, a brush in his hands and Attila at his feet. "No," he said and shook his head when I tried to give him fifteen hundred francs. "You no longer have to."

"You must take it. I'm not coming back, and I don't want you to bother the Kalman family about it."

"I'm sorry about the little boy," he said.

"Why? You didn't drown him, did you? You only scared the living daylights out of him."

"I didn't mean anything bad by it. I only wanted to teach him a lesson. It was a matter of principle."

He looked at the tear on my chest, puzzled. Then he quickly grabbed the money out of my fingers and pushed it into his coat pocket.

"This is not an easy job, you know. People step out of the elevator upstairs and forget to close the door. Before, I didn't care, but nowadays all my blood flows to my feet."

**W**as I guilty of Simcha's death? That question preoccupied me for months. A few times I went to Stadspark, which seemed to me the only place where I might be able to find an answer, any answer. But I found nothing. I even began to question Simcha's existence, perhaps because nowhere else in the city was he as emphatically absent as there.

I looked at the pond from a distance, I walked along the edge of the pond, I bent over the pond, and came to only one conclusion. If my guilt existed, then it was no different from the guilt of the water, the weeping willows, and the ducks in the pond among which I could find none with red sidecurls. They were accomplices, each according to its nature: the water because it couldn't do anything but envelop him, the trees because they had been forced to watch, the ducks because they had lured him with their quacking. And I? I too had followed my nature and had done what was unavoidable. I had loved Simcha Kalman.

Although I passed my examinations and was admitted to the second year of college, I sold my philosophy books and signed up for courses in physics. That delighted my father. From then on, he paid for my apartment so that I could devote myself completely to my studies. I believe that the summer weather lasted well into October that year, but I can't be sure because it was so long ago. I do remember exactly the morning I walked to the university to attend my first physics lecture. The stoops had been scrubbed clean, the sky was shining blue. Heaven and Earth seemed as fresh as on the day of their creation. With sky above my head and earth under my feet I went on my way but in the opposite direction, back to Genesis.